The Anti-Fan and the Idol

Also From Rachel Van Dyken

Mafia Royals
Royal Bully
Ruthless Princess
Scandalous Prince
Destructive King
Fallen Royal
Broken Crown

Liars, Inc.
Dirty Exes
Dangerous Exes

Covet Series
Stealing Her
Finding Him

Bro Code Series
Co-Ed
Seducing Mrs. Robinson
Avoiding Temptation
The Set-Up

Elite Bratva Brotherhood
Debase

The Players Game Series
Fraternize
Infraction
MVP

The Consequence Series
The Consequence of Loving Colton
The Consequence of Revenge
The Consequence of Seduction
The Consequence of Rejection

Forever
Fall
Eternal
Strung
Capture

The Renwick House Series
The Ugly Duckling Debutante
The Seduction of Sebastian St. James
An Unlikely Alliance
The Redemption of Lord Rawlings
The Devil Duke Takes a Bride

The London Fairy Tales Series
Upon a Midnight Dream
Whispered Music
The Wolf's Pursuit
When Ash Falls

The Seasons of Paleo Series
Savage Winter
Feral Spring

The Wallflower Series (with Leah Sanders)
Waltzing with the Wallflower
Beguiling Bridget
Taming Wilde

The Dark Ones Saga
The Dark Ones
Untouchable Darkness
Dark Surrender
Darkest Temptation
Darkest Sinner

Stand-Alones
Mafia Casanova (with M Robinson)
Hurt: A Collection (with Kristin Vayden and Elyse Faber)

Rip
Compromising Kessen
Every Girl Does It
The Parting Gift (with Leah Sanders)
Divine Uprising
A Crown for Christmas

The Anti-Fan and the Idol

A My Summer in Seoul Novella

By Rachel Van Dyken

1001 DARK NIGHTS
PRESS

The Anti-Fan and the Idol: A My Summer in Seoul Novella
By Rachel Van Dyken

Copyright 2022 Rachel Van Dyken
ISBN: 978-1-970077-98-8

Foreword: Copyright 2014 M. J. Rose

Published by 1001 Dark Nights Press, an imprint of Evil Eye Concepts,
Incorporated

Sign up for the 1001 Dark Nights Newsletter
and be entered to win a Tiffany Key necklace.

There's a contest every month!

Go to www.1001DarkNights.com to subscribe.

As a bonus, all subscribers can download
FIVE FREE exclusive books!

Acknowledgments from the Author

I thank God every day I get to do this job, thank you for taking time to read! Thank you so much to 1001 Dark Nights for always being so amazing when it comes to their stories and how they let us authors embark on different journeys every time! I'm so thankful to my readers as well, who keep coming back and who have taken a chance on a slightly different sort of trope that truly brings awareness to a culture and musical phenomenon. To my sensitivity readers—I really appreciate how closely you work with me and how honest you are when it comes to my research and questions. Jill, you're amazing. I'm so lucky to have you as my assistant. Nicole and Nina, so glad we're a team. And Rachel's New Rockin Readers—I freaking love you guys!

One Thousand and One Dark Nights

Once upon a time, in the future…

*I was a student fascinated with stories and learning.
I studied philosophy, poetry, history, the occult, and
the art and science of love and magic. I had a vast
library at my father's home and collected thousands
of volumes of fantastic tales.*

*I learned all about ancient races and bygone
times. About myths and legends and dreams of all
people through the millennium. And the more I read
the stronger my imagination grew until I discovered
that I was able to travel into the stories… to actually
become part of them.*

*I wish I could say that I listened to my teacher
and respected my gift, as I ought to have. If I had, I
would not be telling you this tale now.
But I was foolhardy and confused, showing off
with bravery.*

*One afternoon, curious about the myth of the
Arabian Nights, I traveled back to ancient Persia to
see for myself if it was true that every day Shahryar
(Persian: شهريار, "king") married a new virgin, and then
sent yesterday's wife to be beheaded. It was written
and I had read that by the time he met Scheherazade,
the vizier's daughter, he'd killed one thousand
women.*

Something went wrong with my efforts. I arrived in the midst of the story and somehow exchanged places with Scheherazade – a phenomena that had never occurred before and that still to this day, I cannot explain.

Now I am trapped in that ancient past. I have taken on Scheherazade's life and the only way I can protect myself and stay alive is to do what she did to protect herself and stay alive.

Every night the King calls for me and listens as I spin tales. And when the evening ends and dawn breaks, I stop at a point that leaves him breathless and yearning for more. And so the King spares my life for one more day, so that he might hear the rest of my dark tale.

As soon as I finish a story... I begin a new one... like the one that you, dear reader, have before you now.

Chapter One

Ah-Ri

I stare at myself in the mirror. My eyes are lifeless, and my body feels hollow as my stomach growls. I want food so bad it's all I can think about. I squeeze my eyes shut again and brace my palms against the sink.

I have no choice.

Being from the States with an American mom and a Korean dad doesn't actually help me in this situation, even though I've always thought of myself as Korean.

The only reason we went to LA was because of my dad's job, and I only stayed there for six years before coming back home.

It was enough, though.

Enough to make me different. Enough to make people look at me funny during school and ask why my Korean sounded a bit strange.

Enough for people during my idol training to judge me, though I don't know why. Then again, that's the job, right? Everyone competing for a few spots at the label and dying to make it—literally.

I don't look much different from everyone else, yet I somehow feel ostracized. I grip the sink with both hands and stare down at my black fingernails. My perfect skin and the flawless makeup on my face as my jet-black hair falls in easy waves down past my shoulders.

I have a crop top on with a pair of joggers and black Jordans. I'm trying to go for the cute-but-casual look for this audition.

My seventh.

I've yet to make it into a group, and with the audition only two days away, I need to work harder than I've ever worked before.

It's been my dream since I was five and saw my favorite K-pop group on TV. I became obsessed and begged my parents for voice lessons, dance classes, and everything and anything else that would help me.

Once we moved back to Korea, I finally saw my chance.

Five years later, I'm still waiting for it.

At nineteen, I almost feel like my dreams are out of reach, mainly because I'm getting older, and it seems everyone else is getting younger. They always pass me by because I lack *something* that everyone else seems to possess. I get good marks, people love my dancing, they love my singing and raspy voice, and they even love my hard-working attitude. I just don't get why I can't actually make it. I'm fluent in both Korean and English—and now I feel like I'm bragging in my head. But it's so frustrating. The only thing I can think of is that I'm not as small as everyone else, which makes me want to cry even harder.

I miss burgers.

I take a deep breath and leave the bathroom, head held high. Tons of trainees run down the halls and stop at one of the practice rooms to the right.

I almost laugh because I don't even need to peer into the window to know it's SWT, one of the biggest K-pop groups in the world. They always have people watching them, copying them, dying to meet them, touch them, lick their sweat off the floor.

I trained with their youngest, Sookie, for a year before they picked him up, and he debuted with them.

His tattoos are probably stressing the entire label out. Add in the new piercings, and I'm sure the higher-ups are on full DEFCON mode. His squeaky-clean image no longer looks so squeaky clean…then again, he's the one who got me drunk on my birthday.

I make a mental note to text him later. He's been pretty busy, but he always has time for his friends. I respect that he goes against the grain and that he's his own person, not controlled by the label as much as the rest of the trainees and groups are. He's beautiful. Talented. Amazing.

And one of the nicest people in the industry.

I keep walking as the trainees wall-stalk members of SWT and go to the next practice room. It's empty, which is exactly what I need.

Practice.

I open the door and let it click shut behind me, then grab my cell. Linking it to the speakers, I put on a song from Blackpink and start to dance.

The music comes over me as I move, roll my hips, and practice everything I'll need for my final audition Friday.

Final.

Shit, it really *does* feel final, doesn't it? Because if I can't debut now, what will I do? Take my exams? Work? Go to college? Would I even get in with sub-par test scores?

I stumble through the last few bits of choreography then collapse onto the floor.

Clapping sounds around me.

I look over my shoulder.

It's *him*.

My nemesis.

Haneul.

One of the most hated guys in my universe.

The one who'd told me he'd never kiss someone like me, let alone touch me, after we were both trying out for the same acting gig for a small romantic role in a K-Drama. I obviously didn't get it, and neither did he, but I still remember the poisonous words at the audition when I was already super nervous to even be there.

Ever since then, I've held a grudge—okay, like a huge grudge, even two years later—for him being such a giant dick to me. I may have shoved him and embarrassed him in front of the other trainees auditioning at the label, which he clearly never forgave me for.

Rumors spread about our hatred, and while I always felt guilty for reacting that way, he'd hurt my pride, and I figured I'd hurt his. There was no way I would stay in the same room with him, let alone breathe the same air, unless he was on his hands and knees begging for forgiveness. And I had a small suspicion he thought the same about me.

He's beautiful, though. Like a poisonous flower from *Alice in Wonderland* that promises you'll get everything, only to leave you dead.

I loathe him and everything he represents in the industry. With his rich parents and good looks, he could do anything.

Everyone's obsessed with him. His solo career at the label took off four years ago, and he's been this perfect angel—devil if you ask me—ever since.

"What are you doing here?" I ask.

He shrugs. "I was practicing. Then I got distracted by you."

"You should have said something." I get to my feet and start walking away.

"Wait," he says slowly, calmly, almost in a sexual way...if that's even possible.

I look over my shoulder and drink him in. His hair's a light blond, his eyes blue—most likely contacts. His pink lips are a perfect pout. He's put on some weight, and it looks good on him; he's not as skinny as he was for his debut. I notice a small tattoo on his right hand and then one on his left biceps—not that I'm checking him out or anything.

"What?" I bark. "I'm busy."

"That's funny." He laughs.

"What?"

"You're not busy. You haven't even debuted yet."

I hate his words. I hate his truth. I hate his stupid Gucci bag!

I glare. "Is that all?"

He smiles. "Do you want it to be?"

I grumble "*ass*" under my breath and start walking out again, only to have someone shove the door open, revealing his best friend and bandmate, Ryan.

Two years ago, the label put both solo acts in a group with two other guys to create some sort of supergroup. They've been selling like crazy and getting close to SWT's sales records.

Rumor has it they had a falling out and are about to disband, but who knows? People like to talk in this industry.

Shoot.

God did not prepare me for this day or their lethal beauty.

Haneul smirks in my direction, his smile wide and sexy. For one brief moment, I forget how much I despise him. How do you hate something so nice to look at? I quickly avert my eyes and sadly realize that I'm now looking at Ryan.

Shit.

While Haneul looks light and happy, though still ready to seduce a houseplant, Ryan's anything but.

He grew up in Korea, moved to Canada when his parents divorced, and then returned to train.

Nobody really knows about his background other than he looks like a fallen angel.

I don't even want to know how much money he's made from skincare lines alone. I *do* know he's loaded because of his tech-company-owning father and that he has an attitude issue with authority, though every fan denies it since his smile seems so nice.

I don't know him well. He rarely talks to people, but his pensive look is enough. He's Haneul's best friend and pretty much ignores me when I'm in the room. A year ago, I was doing another audition for the label to possibly make it into a girl group, and while my dancing was completely on point, he was whispering to Haneul the entire time, watching me, throwing me off my game, and smirking. I didn't think a ton about it until I walked out to grab some water and heard him talking with another one of the guys that was trying out for a group next.

"She's pretty," he said.

Ryan made a face. "She's okay, I guess. I was too busy staring at the shit footwork and the fact that she's bigger than the rest of the girls. They won't pick her even if she's the best dancer there. Fans will complain that she stands out when she needs to blend in. It sucks, but it's the truth. At this point, it's almost embarrassing. She should just quit."

"That's harsh," the other trainee said. "Even for you."

Ryan took a sip from his water bottle. "Life's tough, and you know how this industry is. It's better to just face reality—fuck, now I sound like my dad."

They both laughed and turned to me.

I felt the embarrassment all over. It didn't help that both Ryan and the other nameless trainee were drop-dead gorgeous and the envy of everyone at the label. A few girls walked by and started whispering.

I think what I hated the most was that he was right.

I was all wrong.

And he'd pointed it out to someone else.

See? Dicks. Both of them.

"Ryan." I barely get his name out before trying to sidestep his angry, inquisitive stare.

But he suddenly grabs me by the arm and spins me around, backing me against the door. It clicks shut, sealing me in with both bullies.

We're nearly chest to chest. Ryan's taller, so all I can see are his full lips, strong jaw, and long, jet-black hair that caresses his shoulders. I smell his sinful, near-perfect cologne. His white shirt hugs a muscular chest as his fingers dig into both my arms, and he pins me against the door with his body like he has a right to.

"You ask her?" he says in Korean to Haneul without turning around. Is he watching me? Looking down?

Slowly, I lift my gaze.

His brown eyes lock on mine. It's like a tractor-beam pulling me in. I don't even think I blink as I stare back, powerless, allowing my body to respond to his warmth, his larger presence.

His well-known magnetism that's made him so many fans.

"Didn't get a chance," Haneul replies. "She was doing the usual, running off scared, tail between those long"—he looks down—"pretty little legs thing."

Embarrassed, I try to jerk away.

Ryan holds me firm. "We aren't done talking business."

"What are you?" I laugh nervously. "A Triad crime family instead of an idol group?"

He flinches at the mafia reference. "We're doing something different. Under new management. Same label, just…different."

"Good for you," I say slowly. "Can I go now?"

"Two guys, two girls," Ryan says quietly. "Us and…"

"And?" I'm a bit shocked. I only know of one group that's successfully done that. "Who else do you have? And why does this concern me exactly?"

They're both silent.

Someone knocks on the door, and then more trainees start stopping by, waving at the guys. Yeah, I guess they're famous, but they're still a newer group, even though it's been two years.

Doesn't matter, they're both well known for their solo careers, too, and people want what they have.

They want what they see—the perfect idol life.

Which doesn't exist. But that doesn't keep people from trying to obtain it. Just like air. It's there, but you can't grasp it in your hand for longer than a second before it disappears, and you're back to square one.

The fans will most likely bombard both guys and follow them the entire way back to the talent apartments. They'll have already figured out the guys' schedules by now, even though they constantly change them to prevent issues with the sasaeng. Those fans are absolutely terrifying and will stop at nothing to stalk their favorite idols.

Honestly, the biggest question at this point is why I'm getting pinned against the wall by Ryan as Haneul watches.

"Look…" Ryan releases me, but I still feel his thumbprint on my pulse. The sensation travels through my body like a searing drug that may just kill me dead if I give in to the madness of how good it feels. "We need one more girl."

I freeze. Is he saying what I think he is? I almost stop breathing. "And—?"

"You," he says finally. "You're good, you don't take any bullshit, and we need to move fast. Momentum from—"

He stops talking.

Haneul looks away and curses, running his hands through his hair.

"Is One21 disbanding?" I ask.

They both pale.

Holy shit.

My jaw drops.

"It's not what you think, though," Haneul says, though I can see in his gaze that it isn't exactly good news. Which means they have a plan and must have had one for way longer than this conversation.

Ryan jerks his head at Haneul. "Think about it, Ah-Ri. All right? We'll give you a day."

"A *day*?" I nearly shriek. "And I don't even have your phone—hey, what are you doing?"

He walks away and goes to the floor where I left my cell. He grabs it and then hands it to me. "Your passcode?"

I type it in with numb fingers and hold it out.

He puts in his number, then smirks and hands it back. Hey, at least he didn't throw it at my head. I'm almost upset I have no reason to knee him in the balls like last time when he insulted me behind my back.

I glance at the screen. I have no time to process the name he typed in as his contact. I shake my head. Does the arrogance never end with this guy? What? Like he's so much better than me? My insecurity screams, *"Um, yes, he is, because he has a job and you're still failing!"* Why the hell did he give me his number?

And why am I still staring at the screen while the practice door opens and closes with a click. It's like I'm unable to move or believe what just happened.

I shake my head. His name in my phone isn't his name at all, but what I call him behind his back, only he added something special.

It's *Fallen Angel Forever*.

And I wonder if it's a bad omen.

Or good.

Maybe both.

Crap.

Chapter Two

Ah-Ri

"I hate them. I hate them. I hate them."

I don't mean to say it aloud as I grab a bottle of water, stare at my stupid bank card, and realize I have about ten dollars—or, basically, no money to my name.

I think about calling my parents, but they said that if I wanted this, I had to do it on my own. And if I failed...

College. A real job.

Life.

As if this isn't one of the hardest jobs in the world.

Not only did I study until ten every night to finish school, but I had dance practice on top of voice training.

Thank God I didn't need English lessons. Though I was told that if I actually debuted, I'd have to learn Chinese at the very least, which is such an umbrella concept since there are so many dialects.

Insert panic here.

Though, at the moment, I'm probably going to end up working in an office—that is, if I can even complete my college exams.

It's almost laughable that I would ever be able to get into Seoul University. Maybe I could apply overseas.

Back in LA?

I frown, grab my bank card from the ATM, and start stubbornly stomping down the street as it starts to rain.

I mean, why sunshine when I'm having such a great day?

I keep thinking about the guys' proposal.

Why me, of all people? Someone they don't even like.

Why?

They never explained, which makes me even more nervous. They've always despised me, challenged me. And, yes, I've screamed their names in extremely unhealthy ways into my pillow on several occasions. I'm sure other girls scream for other reasons.

I grunt and stop walking. As if they're really *that* good-looking.

I'm completely lying to myself but it does make me feel better.

I shake my head and try not to focus on the fact that, yes, they are. They're that good-looking *and* talented. I frown.

Why is their group disbanding in the first place? They've only been together officially for a short time and have already made a crapton of money.

Did they get caught up in a scandal? Did the other two members, who nobody's heard from in the last few months? Normally, the Netizens are all over it. Those internet sleuths are scary good at finding out information, but I haven't heard anything, and I would like to think I'd be one of the first since I'm a trainee at the same label even if I haven't debuted yet. However, that doesn't mean the gossip doesn't run rampant in this place.

I look to my right and sigh. Ramyeon from the store it is again.

I shake off the rain and go inside to pick out my noodles, strolling down the aisle until I come to the brand I like: Shin Raymun.

Not only does it taste good, but it's also cheap, and I need cheap right now if I want to eat for the rest of the week.

I almost snort because someone told me just yesterday that I still need to lose weight, even though my clothes are hanging off my body at this point.

Apparently, if I look bigger on camera than any of the guys who are training for other groups—even though I'm not competing with them— I'm undesirable. And they're fighting their own battles with trying to look thin and have the perfect jawline and visuals.

Really, I think I'm just feeling sorry for myself. It doesn't help that it completely mystifies me as to why the guys want to add me to their group.

I grab my ramyeon, add water, the egg, and put it in the microwave. Then I go over to a seat by the window in the small store.

This isn't how I saw my glamorous, hard-working life as a trainee going.

The microwave dings. The noodles are too hot to eat, so I sit there and look at his name in my phone as if this choice will one hundred percent cause me to be just as fallen as Ryan.

I stare at the screen for a long time, and then my phone rings.

"Dad." I answer and smile. It's so great how supportive he's been of my dream.

"Have you seen your phone bill?" he asks before I can say anything else. "You need to start paying for this. You're nineteen, Ah-Ri. We've let you do your thing because we believe in you, but you have to do better. We also got a bill for your credit card. When did you even take a credit card out?"

I want to say, "*When I had no money for food or clothes,*" but I keep it in. "I'm sorry. Once I debut, I can pay you back—"

He's quiet for way too long. "I love you…you're my only daughter. But you can't be that naïve to think that you'll even get paid right away or be successful. Some idols wait years to get their first check, and you're going to somehow pay off over a thousand won? With what job? What paycheck?"

I want to say that I could always illegally sell myself on the streets or become a table girl, but I keep it in. Barely. I have to bite my lip until it hurts so I don't blurt out something disrespectful or inappropriate.

I sigh. "I have a new opportunity. It's a bit different, but…"

He pauses. "No. I want you to marry for love like I did."

I laugh. "Appa! It's not that!"

"Then how? What? I'm trying to understand. And why aren't you back at the dorms yet?"

I stare into my ramyeon and stir it with my plastic fork. "Thinking about this new opportunity, that's all."

He's quiet, thinking. Pensive. "Will you be able to debut? Follow your dream?"

I nod before answering. "Yeah, probably. Yes."

I can practically hear his pride and excitement through the phone. "Then you take it. You take it hard, you perform hard, but you take it."

"No matter the idols I'm with?" I ask casually.

"No matter how mean those girls can be."

Ha! Guys. But, okay, sure. Perfect.

"You take your dream with both hands, Ah-Ri."

Tears well in my eyes. "I'll find a way to pay my phone bill."

"Take your dreams with both hands, and I'll pay it for you," he says softly. "Just don't say no to an opportunity to do what you love if you have it right in front of you."

A tear slides down my cheek. "Okay, I'll be home soon to have dinner with you guys."

"Are you hungry?"

I stare down at the ramyeon and lie. I'm already insecure enough about my body, and I know he's doing it to celebrate. Unfortunately, right now, I have to do this alone, as he said. Need to use the only money I have to eat dinner. Both hands, right? Both hands. "Stuffed, actually."

"Mom just grilled some meat. Come over now. Don't be late," he says before hanging up. The line disconnects. I know I'll have to take the bus to their house, then sit in front of them and listen to more lecturing, and I hate it. But I *am* still hungry. Why is this all so hard?

I wipe my cheeks, then scroll through my phone.

My fingers tremble as I stop on *Fallen Angel Forever.*

I send the text that will seal my destiny.

My fate.

My forever.

And type two simple words.

I'm. In.

Chapter Three

Ryan

I don't expect her text.

I'm so shocked I stare at my phone for a few minutes before taking a deep breath. Or maybe that's what it feels like to finally breathe a sigh of relief—my first one since all the shit went down a few months ago.

We're at the same label and were given some restrictions on what we could do and a timeline, but we're the label's first to start in a new direction in K-pop—despite there being one other co-ed group in the industry.

Funny thing is, the minute you think you have a genius idea, everyone wants to stop you because it seems like it's too out of the norm.

Haneul and I live in the same apartment we used to live in with the group, except we now have spare bedrooms since the other two members left for the military.

The whole point was to go together.

But they decided to do it without us, disbanding the group right after we started truly taking off with worldwide recognition.

And now it's back to ground zero.

You can't really be a K-pop group with two rappers. I mean, you *could*, but that wasn't the look we had from management.

We can sing, but two of us? Who's going to come to see two guys missing their other lead vocalists?

I'm still pissed, honestly.

I'm pissed because things were strained since the beginning with the group. When the label put us in the supergroup, Haneul and I were both solo artists, but the other two guys had already been a part of two groups and had basically grown up together. Shit, talk about creative differences between the four of us. We kept everything behind closed doors, though.

On stage, everything was perfect. Sold-out concerts, millions upon millions of views on our videos. We were trending worldwide when our last mini-album dropped a year ago.

And now? They're gone.

They weren't happy.

They needed a break.

And while I can understand how hard they worked since they were sixteen, and how much traveling and crazy scheduling they had to go through, I'm being selfish. Because while I can sell the hell out of a skincare line, I wanted to be a part of something bigger.

And I thought I'd found that with them.

At least Haneul and I had each other and were able to form a friendship based on utter betrayal and sadness.

Yeah, we had at least four drunken nights in a row once the guys announced they were taking a break and going into the military, leaving Haneul and me with the choice to go back to our solo projects or do something new.

Maybe it was the soju talking, but at two in the morning a month ago, we came up with an idea. What about a group with two guys and two girls? What if we played both sides and pulled in fans from everywhere? Created a new bias for K-pop? I knew of only one group that had successfully done it, and they're still busting ass at another label.

Which brings us to this predicament.

Haneul and I basically told the label that we needed to compete with them if we wanted to stay relevant.

They fucking went for it but didn't want to invest a ton of money or time into it. So, they dropped the entire plan into our laps, gave us a timeline, and that was it. If we do well on the debut stage, get a certain number of views on our music video, and can get on the Billboard charts with our first song, they'll financially back us one hundred percent and actually pay us right out of the gate.

If not?

Game over.

I asked my dad to invest, and he even said he wouldn't make a bet he wasn't sure he could win and would wait and see.

Haneul's dad said the same thing.

So that left us…panicked.

The songs for the mini-album are ready.

The concept for the MV—the music video—is completely drawn out.

And we already have another girl, a rookie who looks nervous every time Haneul or I talk to her, which brings me back to the dark horse. Ah-Ri.

She's got a mouth on her in more ways than one.

And we'll need that attitude.

Plus, she's not just a visual. She can dance, sing, rap—she can do it all. Sure, she's a bit tall, not as thin as some of the other trainees, and is so fucking argumentative I want to slam my head against the wall, but she's really all we've got at this point.

Every other person we approached said they didn't want to take the chance on us and would rather do a variety show before trying a co-ed group.

I go knock on Haneul's door and wait for him to answer. Finally, he pulls it open, his blond hair messy around his face, blue contacts out, and his brown eyes showing. He's wearing a Nike shirt and joggers and looks like he's just waiting for disappointment.

"So…" I gulp. "She texted."

"Let me guess." He sighs. "A giant middle finger followed by a shit emoji?"

"Not exactly…" I lift my phone and show it to him.

He looks ready to pass out as he grabs it. "Is this a prank?"

"Nah." I shove my hands into my pockets. "She's in."

"So, we have a group!" Haneul says. "We have a fucking group!"

I smile; I can't help it. "We have a group."

His smile suddenly falters. "That means we need to get our schedules figured out. The songs are already written. They'll need to learn them and the choreography. Why don't we divide and conquer at first? I'll work with Jisoo, and you can work with Ah-Ri separately for the next two weeks. Then we'll combine and do all the joint tracks and choreo."

"Wait, why do I get Ah-Ri?"

"Because." He smiles. "I might actually murder her if I'm in the same room with her and her smart mouth for longer than zero seconds."

"That's not even mathematically possible."

"Exactly. Because it's *not* possible." He snorts. "Look, maybe you can soften her up a bit so I don't go to prison when we start our joint practice sessions."

"Murder's a death sentence in Korea."

He hands my phone back and smirks. "So, I guess you're saving my life in a way."

My thoughts go to her smart mouth and shit attitude, and then I'm thinking about her outfit, the sweat running down her cheeks, and the way her skin glistened under the lights.

I hate her, I remind myself, but only because the alternative is acknowledging the major crush that I've had on her ever since watching her dance. My hate is all I have, and it's mostly directed at myself for hurting her feelings. For being *that guy*.

The truth is, I hate myself.

And it's too hard to look in the mirror and take responsibility for the fact that I can't even look at another girl. I can't date. It's always been her. It's easier for me to blame her for my inability to even look at others than take responsibility.

Ah, Dad would be so proud.

Besides, crushing on a girl about to be in our new group isn't the best idea I've ever had, so I hold onto the hate, even though it's childish and immature.

This is business.

Survival.

This is years of working our asses off and getting betrayed by our bandmates.

And I'm not a good actor. I'd get eaten alive in any K-Drama—fully.

If I can pull this off, I can start writing for other artists, maybe producing—which is the real dream. One day I want to start my own label that offers idols more freedom and doesn't involve falling for the one girl who has the power to get in my way and distract me—even if she is good.

I swallow the lump of anger and frustration in my throat and nod. "Fine, I'll text her later and book some of the practice rooms for the next few weeks."

Haneul shrugs. "At least you're good at pretending. I can't do it, not with her. Plus, you debuted early and were already successful on your own before joining a group. How hard can this be?"

How hard, indeed.

"I guess we'll see," I grumble.

"Cool, I'll call Jisoo now." He shuts the door, and I walk on numb legs into the main room to sit on one of the couches.

I drop my phone onto the table and stare down at it.

I don't realize my hands are shaking until my text alert goes off again, and I see it's another one from Ah-Ri.

Ah-Ri: *So? Do you have a plan?*

Fuck. I sure hope so.

Chapter Four

Ah-Ri

He's late.

And I'm annoyed.

He said we should meet at the practice room at six a.m., and I've already been here for a half-hour, waiting for everyone else to show up.

Do we even have a group name?

Songs?

Anything?

When's the debut?

I have so many questions and so much anxiety I want to puke. Instead, I stare at myself in the mirror and truly wonder what part of my brain misfired last night when I said yes.

Other than my parents basically threatening me.

In a loving, albeit figure-yourself-out way.

I take a deep breath. I'm wearing a pair of black leggings, a white crop top, and a long-sleeve red plaid button-up, hanging open in case I get cold—though I'm sure they're about to put every member through hell.

The door to the practice room opens.

I look up and feel even sicker.

It's Ryan.

By himself.

I expect everyone else to shuffle in behind him.

They don't.

This is a problem. Is he going to be cruel with his words again? Is he going to actually play nice? Every insecurity in my arsenal comes flaring back to life, and yet he asked me to be a part of this. Did everyone else turn him down?

"Where is everyone?" I ask.

He drops his bag to the floor and then kicks it toward the wall. "Practicing. Just like us."

My stomach drops. "Why not *with* us?"

He won't meet my eyes. He has his dark hair pulled back from his face and a black Yankees hat on.

In fact, he's in all black right now.

Black sweats, black shirt, black hat.

Totally gives dancing with the devil a new meaning.

"Because." He goes over to the sound system and taps away on his iPhone. Music starts pouring through the room.

The beat is fast.

And it starts off right away.

Electric.

Different.

I like it.

It feels fresh.

He sets his phone down. "The plan is to divide and conquer right now. We have next to no time, and no group ever gets this kind of freedom from the label, so we have to prove ourselves worthy of that freedom."

Something trickles down my spine. "And why exactly are they letting you guys take the lead? That's not typical. In fact, it's not just rare, it's—"

"I know what it is," Ryan snaps in that smooth voice of his. Damn, it matches his skin, doesn't it? Perfect perfection wrapped in a grumpy attitude. "And it's none of your business why. Just say 'thank you' and get your ass to work."

I suddenly realize that he's speaking in English.

I've gotten so used to talking in Korean that I'm confused why he's switched it up on me.

"Fine," I say in Korean.

He gives me a funny look but keeps talking as if I haven't said anything. "We have six singles, all written. Each girl gets a part in each song, and we're trying to make it even. Haneul choreographed the dance sequences, so they're not exactly going to be easy."

"Me, either," I say, then realize what I just said and backpedal. "I mean that I'm good at dancing, not that I'm easy. My brain didn't go there. I was just—"

"Stop talking," he snaps. "It's embarrassing for both of us."

He moves to the middle of the room.

I cross my arms in annoyance and get even more annoyed when he shows me the choreography. It's good. Like really, *really* good.

And hard.

I hold my head high.

This is it.

My last chance.

And why am I singing *Last Dance* in my head now?

Ryan rolls his hips and then drops to the wood floor.

My jaw also drops as his hips press against it. He flips around to his back and then jumps up. I'm so entranced that I can't peel my eyes away from his body.

He's using the entire floor, completely dominating every inch of space as he moves across it, utterly owning the song and how his body moves.

Sweat trickles down his cheek, sliding past his sculpted jawline and onto his black shirt. He turns to me once the song ends, then pulls off his tee and wipes his face.

My nerves are on fire as I try not to stare at his perfectly lean body, his six-pack—no, wait, is that even six? Seven? Eight?

I put my hands on my hips so he thinks I'm annoyed and unimpressed. In reality, my heart is slamming against my chest so hard it almost hurts to breathe.

"From the top," he says, tossing his shirt to the floor.

"And here I thought Canadians were supposed to be super nice and polite," I mutter.

"And here *I* thought Korean-Americans had something to prove." He jabs right back where it decimates me.

As if he knows how hard I've tried.

And how much I feel like I'll never fit in.

Maybe it's all self-sabotage. It's not like anyone's been anything but nice to me. Accepting.

They're my insecurities.

I realize that.

It's me.

I'm the problem.

I'm the one with the chip on my shoulder because I want to be like everyone else.

And I won't ever be anything but someone who lacks star potential.

"Stop." He grabs me by the shoulders. "See, that's your problem."

"W-what?" I jerk away.

He grabs me again. "You think too much. You need to feel."

"Or maybe I feel too much and think too little," I counter.

His smirk is devastating as he jerks me close to him. "Maybe you should just focus on the feeling."

His chest is inches from mine.

My breath hitches as his full mouth lowers, his lips nearly caressing my ear as he whispers, "Feel me."

"What?" I don't mean to shriek; it just happens.

His chuckle is dark and delicious, like a single bite of chocolate cake you don't even want to swallow because it tastes like heaven on your tongue.

"Feel." He spins me around until I face the mirror. His hands glide from my shoulders down my body. "Just feel before we start with all the counting, the steps, the movement. Because the song is about feeling, emotion…" His voice lowers. "Sex."

I gasp, a bit horrified because while I know it sometimes happens between trainees, it is literally never spoken about aloud. "Is that even allowed?"

He smirks in the mirror. "It's not like we spell it out, but the hints are there. So, you need to feel. You need to empower the people watching you to feel. And you need to make them believe it, even if you want to strangle me. We're doing something different."

I gulp, then nod my head. My entire body is a live wire as I stand there, staring at myself in the mirror. Finally, I close my eyes. The song starts again. Without realizing it, I'm swaying. Moving.

Ryan stays behind me.

I can feel his body heat and hear his breaths. I could probably count his heartbeats if I were closer.

The song finds its ending.

My eyes flash open.

He stares at me through the mirror. "Ready?"

"Ready," I say.

Five hours later, with one break for coffee and a protein bar, my body hurts so bad I want to live in a hot tub. I'm starving and want real food but really haven't had anything outside of ramyeon and vegetables for years, so why change now?

I swear my body's crying for more.

But I'm still bigger than anyone else.

Taller.

I'm still not right.

My stomach growls when I go to get my stuff.

Ryan, of course, just happens to be right next to me, grabbing his bag.

He picks it up and says nothing.

Embarrassed, I grab mine and follow him out.

"You did okay for your first day," he says without looking back. "Tomorrow, you'll work on your part of the song and do another round of choreography."

I run to catch up with him. "How long do we have to get this all down?"

He stops, and I nearly run into him.

His head hangs. "We have four weeks until our Showcase."

"What!?" I shriek. "That's impossible! Like literally impossible!"

"We don't have a choice. The label gave us that long. It took us a while to find people willing, and"—he shakes his head—"you wouldn't understand."

"Understand what?" I ask. "Why not give us more time?"

"Because they want us to fucking fail!" Ryan shouts, finally turning around. "Don't you see? We're doing something different. We're trying to break out of an industry that wants you to stay the same over and over again. Perfect skin, perfect bodies, perfect clothes, perfect smiles for your fans. I want to do something different, and so does Haneul. And if this label's willing to give us that chance, we need to take it. Who knows when or if we'll get it again?"

I'm stunned and left speechless for a minute. "Wait, so they're really letting you take the full reins on this? From clothing to diets to—?"

"It's just Haneul and me—and now you and Jisoo."

It's just us.

I swallow the dryness building up in my throat. "And if we fail?"

Ryan's gaze is sharp. "We can't."

"But if we do?"

"Are you not hearing me?" He slams his hands against the wall next to him. "We. Can't. Fail. If we do, you'll be working at Subway. Nothing against sandwiches, but we can't fail. Do you understand what I'm saying?"

I squeeze my eyes shut. He's so mean. And yet, at the same time, I appreciate the honesty.

No honeyed words.

Not even any promises.

This industry will beat you down until you don't even recognize yourself anymore. He knows it.

He has a story, too.

I'm afraid to ask.

Because it might make me run.

"Okay." I nod. "I get it. Don't become a sandwich artist before twenty over a failed group."

He puts his hand on my head and shoves me away a bit playfully.

Some might see his attitude as cruel, but I know it's more like, *yeah, we're all in this together.*

And now I'm singing *High School Musical* in my head.

Perfect.

"Good." He turns and keeps walking. "Six a.m. Make sure your vocals are warm."

"Am I singing a solo or—?"

He looks over his shoulder and grins. "I'd like to think of it as a duet."

"I was afraid of that," I mutter.

"Get some rest." He nods. "Oh, and when we pull this off, make sure to be nice to Jisoo. She sneezes when she's nervous."

"Seriously?"

He shrugs. "She's nice."

"And I'm not?"

He doesn't say anything, just keeps walking, making me wonder until the early hours of the morning what Ryan thinks of me and why I actually care.

Chapter Five

Ryan

Everything feels different as I wait for Ah-Ri in the studio. I find myself looking for her for no reason other than to make sure I can see the sour expression on her face every time I make her do something she doesn't want to do.

I know she works hard.

I also know she hates me after what I said about her. She just doesn't know why I felt compelled to say it. I was petrified that rumors would spread about me liking her, and I'd get into trouble or lose things I'd worked for. And worse? I *did* actually like her, and I didn't want her getting into trouble either. Dating isn't just frowned upon; you either sneak around and put everything on the line, hoping you don't get caught…

Or you get caught and get into trouble.

I get why anything teamwork related makes her even angrier.

But after yesterday, she has to know how important this is.

I know she's never been my fan.

Hell, anyone who speaks to her knows that Haneul and I are basically her worst nightmares. We both insulted her and made her feel small. I did it because I was crushing on her and because of my own stupid fear, and he did it because he was jealous that she got higher marks on her dance routine one time, which just turned into this weird competitive thing when he went to an audition with her.

After a shit ton of soju, he finally confessed that he was nervous about the kissing scene and was afraid he'd do it wrong for his first acting audition. So, he just reacted.

That was a couple of years ago, and after she insulted him in front of everyone, well…it just made him even more resolute. I knew telling my best friend that I had a crush on his mortal enemy wouldn't go over well, so I just went along with it, to protect her and, yes, myself.

The fact is, no one else was as talented and willing to go against everything in the industry.

No one.

Believe me, I checked.

I glance at my phone again.

She's not late.

Yet.

My dad still hasn't texted me back since hearing about this challenge of forming a group. And if I see another breaking news story about my dad's company and how well they're doing, I might actually puke before I can record. The articles almost always show a picture of my perfectly happy-yet-tortured face as I stand next to my dad, knowing that I'm only there for a photo op—that being an idol is the exact opposite of what he wanted for my life.

I drink more hot tea and lean back in my chair.

If this day goes anything like yesterday, it will be long.

Haneul was all smiles when he got back to the apartment. He said that Jisoo was a dream to work with and listened to everything he said.

I almost laughed.

If his day was perfect, my experience was painful.

Why does Ah-Ri have to ask so many questions?

Why does she need explanations for everything?

Sure, if we fail, she's screwed, but I'm still offering her something huge. And she hasn't even said thank you.

If her voice isn't that good, I swear I'll headbutt the sound room until nothing's left but the echoes of my screams.

It's been a while, and back then, she was still taking voice lessons. All I remember is going, *hmm that's nice.*

She has a raspy voice.

Different than others.

Lower.

Not as trendy.

But I like it.

Or I liked it back then.

Who knows what she can do now?

The door to the studio opens.

She runs in wearing a pair of low-slung baggy jeans and a white cropped sweatshirt, showing off her toned body.

I frown.

Suddenly, I'm more concerned about breakfast than her singing.

Did she eat?

For being so tall, she's thin. Too thin.

I frown harder.

She's pale, too.

"Did you eat?" I ask, my voice cracking.

She stops in her tracks and chews her bottom lip as if she wants to eat but can't. She touches her stomach as it growls. "I can eat later."

"No," I snap. "You have to eat. You shouldn't starve yourself. You're tall, you should have curves with that body. Keep them, let everyone be jealous of them for all I care. But you need nutrition. Energy. You need food." I shove the chair away from me. "Damn it, you need to eat!" I start pacing. "What's wrong with you?"

"Why are you making this personal?" Tears well in her eyes. "I'm fine!"

"You're not fine, Sari!" I yell, then squeeze my eyes closed. "I mean, Ah-Ri."

"Sari?" She repeats and slumps to the chair across from me. "She died last—"

"I know," I whisper.

"You need to eat, Sari. You're too thin; your body needs food," I whisper, hugging her close, hoping to comfort her.

She laughs. "I'll be fine. Stop worrying so much, it's annoying." She smiles at me again. "Everything's fine!"

I feel the lies in the air.

And I let her keep giving them.

Two weeks later, she was gone.

Dead.

After jumping from a bridge.

She was twenty and had just gotten her first acting job.

Her letter was made out to me.

She died hungry. She died sad. She died alone.

And it was all my fault.

I saw the signs and stupidly believed the lies because I was choking down the same ones.

Some labels care for their idols.

And others, like hers, just want to make money.

She died alone.

Without me.

"Here." I thrust a protein bar into Ah-Ri's face. "I'll order us some food before we start. Keep warming up your voice."

An hour later, we've both eaten. Ah-Ri looked nervous to put the food past her lips, and I hate that it's normal for trainees to diet so severely. Last year, two of the girls from a debut group were hospitalized for malnourishment.

The worst part is, I know that our label is actually more lenient than others.

It's the fans—not that I would ever admit that out loud. We have some incredible ones, but there are always some who think they can dictate everything you do from what you wear to what you eat, even down to your ability to date.

I shove the food away. "You ready?"

Ah-Ri nods, putting her hands against her stomach. Was it the food? Or is she just nervous?

I play the song for her only once, thinking we'll be listening to it over and over again so she can learn her part.

Most of it's in Korean except for the chorus.

I want you, need you, have you, had you but lost. Pick up the pieces of the broken glass you tossed. Make it better, heal me, find me, make us stronger. Maybe it was never me but you that was the problem.

The chorus comes in.

Ah-Ri listens intently.

"The next verse is you," I say as it starts.

Her smile is small at first and then grows so wide I can't look away. She nods her head to the music, then closes her eyes, allowing me to stare even more.

She's beautiful.

No, that's not right. The music and the way she responds to it is beautiful. That's what my soul recognizes. And, deep down, despite all the fake confidence and money…

I want her to like it.

The music.

The choreography.

The rap lines.

I find myself smiling.

"Stop staring at me, Ryan," she says without opening her eyes.

I cough, clear my throat, and look away, drumming my fingertips on the table in a nervous fashion until the song ends.

She spins toward me in the chair and announces, "I'm ready."

I jump to my feet. "You've only heard it once."

"Yup." She goes to the booth.

"Once," I remind her.

"Caught that." She goes inside and shuts the door, then grabs her headphones.

All right, then.

I go to the soundboard and get ready to layer the tracks, then hit the comm. "You'll just record your solo for now, then we'll see how far we can get on the harmony on the chorus. The others have the booth later today." I exhale. "I left the lyrics in there for you to look at just in case."

She gives me a thumbs-up.

I just shake my head and intro her into the song.

She isn't late.

She's spot-on.

Her eyes close again as she records her solo with professionalism and perfection. Beauty.

"One more take," I say once she's finished.

She rolls her eyes. "That was perfect!"

"Yeah, I can't hear you," I joke.

She raises a middle finger.

"But I can see." I chuckle and count her down again.

I didn't think it was possible, but she does it again—and even better than the first time.

When I stop recording, I look at the clock. We have at least another hour left of studio time.

She comes out of the booth with a knowing smile on her face.

I spin toward her and hang my head, wincing. "You searching for compliments right now? A solid pat on the back?"

She laughs. "Come on, I nailed it!"

I hold out my hand for a high-five. "These are rare, just so you know."

"Your hands?"

"My high-fives," I grumble, trying like hell not to laugh.

She sends her fist flying into my palm.

It stings.

I kind of like it. "Were you afraid our palms would kiss or what?"

A pink blush stains her cheeks. "It's cute, you calling it that. Still waiting for your first real kiss then?"

"Please." I snort.

"You're…what? Twenty-five?" She takes a seat next to me. I scoot farther away, not wanting to have this conversation—like *no* part of it. "But you're also an idol who's been on a tight leash. No dating scandals, no rumors."

I fumble with the soundboard.

I know she's going to ask it.

Haneul's been giving me shit for years about it.

"No girlfriends…boyfriends… Do you even have a cat? A goldfish?"

I let out an annoyed sigh. "I have a cat at the talent apartments."

She slow claps. "How very risky of you. What's its name?"

"Slytherin," I answer quickly. "Now, let's go back into the booth and lay out the chorus so we can beat the other two to it and kick their asses."

She jumps to her feet.

"Oh, so that's how to motivate you. Competition." I laugh.

"I'm doing it for House Slytherin," Ah-Ri says. "Haven't even met your cat, and I'm weirdly already more on his side than yours."

"Everyone always is." My sister used to be obsessed with that cat. My dad's allergic, so I keep it at the talent apartments. He likes to sleep with Haneul, though. Go figure. Even my cat sleeps with other people.

I shudder.

My brain really needs to get off the memory of sleeping with things like a cat so I don't embarrass myself or remember things I swore I'd forget.

I start the music and go into the booth with Ah-Ri. Both of us stand in front of the microphone, and I press the headphones to my ear so I can hear myself better and wait for the chorus to start.

I'm already wondering how she's going to harmonize with me. I haven't given her any direction, wanting to see what she'll do with it. Will she just sing in unison with me?

I count us down with my hands and then point at the chorus part of the sheet I left in the booth.

We both start to sing the chorus, and then she breaks apart from me and takes the higher harmony.

It sounds how I imagined it would, and I want to keep going because it feels good being in here with her, so I motion for her to keep singing her part.

She does it flawlessly.

We hit the chorus again before it goes into my rap line. I get lost in the words. Music always has a way of distracting me. The chorus pops up again.

Ah-Ri joins in and starts to dance a bit next to me.

I smile and keep singing.

We do four more takes, all of them perfect yet slightly different. By the time we finish the last one, I have so much adrenaline pumping through my system that I could record all day.

She pulls off her headphones and holds up her hand.

I make a fist and punch it lightly.

Ah-Ri throws her head back and laughs. "I guess I deserved that."

"You really did." I smirk, then hold up my other hand. "One last chance?"

She sets her headphones on the stand, moves in front of me, and then slowly presses her palm against mine.

Instinct takes over. My fingers slide into hers. Her smile falters as she stares at our joined hands. "Looks like our palms like a seriously long kiss."

"A lingering kiss," I tease, licking my lips.

"Lingering, huh?" Her eyes focus on my mouth.

This is a bad idea, my brain screams. *Do not fall for your bandmate, the very one you could hate later or have to see on tour every day. In the history of bad ideas, this would be the worst.*

Slowly, I pull my hand away from hers.

It falls empty at my side.

It doesn't hurt, but it doesn't feel good, either.

It feels like she's missing when she's standing right in front of me.

She stares down at her hand, then over at mine before slowly grabbing it again and pressing a kiss to my palm.

Her lips burn a hole through my skin. They create a memory with zero effort, one I'll never escape from unless someone chops off my hand.

"You guys alive in there?" Haneul's voice comes through the sound system. I jerk away from Ah-Ri, look through the glass, and leave the booth.

It was a moment of temporary insanity, brought on by high emotions, close proximity, and touching.

No more high-fives.

No more palm kissing.

Am I a toddler or something?

I wipe my hands on my black sweats and casually run a hand through my hair as I walk toward Haneul. Jisoo is in the corner on her phone.

Haneul smirks like he caught me making out.

It was just our hands.

Shit. I need to relax. It's not like he's my dad.

"Problem recording?" Haneul smiles wider.

"Um, no. We killed it." I lean against the board and cross my arms.

"Uh-huh." Haneul reclines in his chair, legs spread like his dick is so big it needs space. "So, everything went great then in that small, tiny, little room? Did you brush up against her too much or what?"

"What the hell are you talking about?"

Haneul bursts out laughing. "I knew I got here early for a reason, and the universe provides!" He points at my cock. "Should probably take care of that before your anti-fan comes out here and finds out that while you may pretend to hate her, your body definitely isn't on the same page." He tilts his head to the right. "Grower not a shower, hmmm?"

I look down.

"Fuck!" I quickly shove my hand in front of my hardening dick. I mean, seriously. Over a high-five? Really? I can't leave without running into Jisoo, and I can't turn around because of Ah-Ri. "Help!"

"I like women." Haneul laughs harder.

"Not like that, you bastard. And you know it!" I grit my teeth. "Distract Jisoo."

He slowly gets to his feet. "Fine, but you owe me. Oh, and we *will* be talking about this later."

"Not if I can help it," I grumble.

Footfalls sound behind me.

Shit. Ah-Ri is coming out of the booth.

She's going to see my boner and think that what we did is all it takes to turn me on. Which I guess is maybe semi-true but not typical. And, hell, she's probably going to faint.

I'm going to make my bandmate faint in shock and horror on day two of rehearsal.

I quickly look around for an escape when Haneul gets Jisoo's attention and leads her to the corner.

I bolt toward the door and hear Ah-Ri say my name.

"Be right back." I don't look back.

I kick open the door and run to the bathroom down the hall, thanking the universe that it's close.

I lock myself in one of the stalls and look down. "You've got to be shitting me!"

Sure, it's been a while.

Like two years since I've even had a random one-night stand.

I've been busy, though!

Really, really, really busy.

I can either stay in the stall until my body calms down or take care of the situation so it doesn't happen again today.

Especially during dance rehearsal.

I never should have let my thoughts go there with Ah-Ri. From here on out, I need to be laser focused. No wondering about her skin or taste or anything even remotely romantic.

I pull my sweatpants down and grip myself. Damn, it feels good— too good. I lean my other hand against the stall and pump up and down my length. My body trembles.

And, of course, as I jack myself...

I see her face.

My teeth clench.

Her hands.

Her singing.

Her mouth.

Before I know it, I'm spilling into my hand, the toilet, and narrowly miss my legs.

I'm panting, standing there feeling guilty as hell.

And the worst part?

I don't think it's going to be my last time having to do this.

Shit.

Chapter Six

Ah-Ri

Jisoo barely said two words to me but was at least nice when I met her at the studio. Apparently, there are plans for all of us to go to the apartment and have our first group dinner tonight.

Though given the way Ryan's been treating me since this morning, I'm wondering if it's a setup so he can push me off the building.

He's been completely opposite what he was like earlier at the studio. Everything I do with the choreography is wrong, to the point where he keeps stopping the music.

"Again." His chest heaves and sweat pours down his face.

I take my position next to him and do the eight count. I spin around him, ending up in front of him. I roll my hips. His hands go there, gripping me so softly I'm confused. He spins me around and slides through my legs—it's the part of the song where he's rapping. He comes back toward me. I'm in perfect sync with him when he grabs me from behind again and rolls our bodies together.

I gasp at how lightly he's holding me.

Now it's my turn to stop the music. "I'm not going to break."

"What?" He snags a towel and wipes his face. "What the hell do you mean?"

"The choreography is going to look like shit if you're afraid to touch me." I put my hands on my hips. "Look, I know I'm not your favorite person in the world, but I thought we were at least making progress."

He sneers and tosses the towel. "You thought wrong."

I knew I shouldn't have trusted those easy smiles in the booth or the teasing; he was just happy that he was getting what he wanted.

Another body to fill the group, one who doesn't suck.

My chest cracks a bit as he ignores me and starts typing away on his phone as if he doesn't even care about me enough to listen.

"Whatever," I grumble. "Just grab me harder. Otherwise, we won't be able to sell the song or the choreography and it will look weak."

He puts his phone away. "Maybe if you stopped messing up—"

"Shut up, Ryan." I turn the music back on and wait for him to join me.

He looks pissed.

When it's time for him to grab me, he jerks my body against his so hard I nearly stumble. I can feel every sweaty inch of him.

Maybe not the best idea I've ever had.

He's all heated muscle under that loose T-shirt.

His right hand splays across my stomach as our hips move in sync. He leans in. I see his reflection in the mirror. I'm in great shape, yet I'm out of breath.

He whispers in my ear. "Is this hard enough for you?"

Why do his words sound dirty and so exciting?

"I've felt harder," I say, pulling away from him, but not before he spins me around and kisses me. He tastes like sweat and sin. My lips part, and he grips my hips, pulls me against him, and continues dancing against me.

I let him. Like an idiot.

When the music suddenly ends, he breaks away from me and smirks. "Was that convincing enough for you, Ah-Ri?"

Tears well in my eyes. My emotions are all over the place. I want him to pull me closer and yet I still want to kick him in the dick. "You're a prick! And I'm too sweet for you. I hope you die from the bitterness of that kiss."

"Says the girl who kissed me back." He towers over me. "Maybe you're more of a fan than you say."

"You're seriously a jerk." I shove him away from me. "Practice is over."

"Guess I'll see you at dinner tonight then."

I swipe at my cheeks with the back of my hand, grab my water bottle and bag, and shove open the door so hard I nearly take someone out on the other side.

It's Sookie.

He smiles, but the smile drops and turns to rage as he looks from my tear-stained cheeks—and most likely swollen mouth—to the non-empty room and a still angry Ryan.

Like he even has a right to be angry!

I feel so stupid and used that I immediately want to quit.

But I'm not a quitter, so I just stand there and try to keep the rest of the tears in.

"Sorry," I say to Sookie in Korean. His English is getting way better, and there are so many bets that he actually understands it but that he just gets nervous about messing up when he uses it.

"Are those tears from him?" he asks.

"Maybe." I cross my arms. "But he's not worth it."

"Did he hurt you?" Sookie goes into immediate big-brother mode.

Only my heart. But I never gave it to him in the first place; the stupid bastard just keeps trying to crack his way in.

Except today he used kindness instead of a hammer.

Lucky me.

Sookie takes a step toward the door. I shake my head. "No."

I glance over my shoulder in time to see Ryan watching us. I read rage in his eyes and don't understand it.

He, of all people, should know about me and Sookie's friendship. And yet he looks ready to punch someone he calls a friend.

Sookie's fists clench at his sides. His tattoos are on full display under a simple white Gucci shirt and sweats. He's clearly here to practice, and now I've ruined that.

SWT has a new album dropping later this year, so the last thing Sookie needs is to get into a fight or involve the group in a scandal.

"Seriously." I touch his arm.

"Stay away from him if you can."

"Yeah, I'll try," I lie. "Now, go practice."

He sighs and then bites out a curse that has me laughing. Yeah, squeaky clean my ass.

He takes off his Supreme hat, plops it on my head, winks, then runs his hands through his light brown hair before walking toward his practice room.

The rest of the guys must already be there since I don't hear screaming coming from the direction I'm walking.

By the time I get back to the dorm to change out of my sweaty clothes, shower, and get ready, I'm so bone-tired that I want to cry, and there's nobody I can really talk to.

I'm still at the trainee dorms the label thankfully rented across the street, and while my room connects to a larger communal area, most of the girls I got close with no longer live here.

A sixteen-year-old moved in last week, which was even more depressing. Basically, I've dedicated my life to becoming an idol, have zero friends I can talk to, and am having boy problems.

And the final cherry on top? If I actually tell any of my friends, it could get out that my new bandmate and I shared an angry kiss, and we'd be screwed before we even begin.

Besides, while the idea of Sookie punching Ryan in the face makes my heart hurt a little less, it would screw with everything.

The Netizens would not be pleased.

Cancel culture is real, and even I don't hate Ryan that much.

I glance around my empty bedroom. So many roommates have moved in and out that even the idea of living with Ryan and Haneul sounds nice at this point. Maybe then I could torture Ryan for making me cry and get away with it.

I touch my lips, shake the exhaustion from my body, put on a simple adidas sweat outfit, and decide last minute to put on the hat that Sookie gave me, even though it doesn't really match.

"Well,"—I look at my reflection in the mirror—"here goes my first group dinner at the devil's house."

I mentally put on the armor I'll need and leave.

Chapter Seven

Ryan

I fucked up.

I know that.

My body knows it.

My brain's still misfiring. Oh, and I want to choke the life out of Sookie, one of my actual friends, who's truly one of the nicest guys in the world and would do anything for me.

Yeah, I want him dead.

Logically, I know he wasn't flirting with Ah-Ri. I know they're friends because I try to change the subject whenever he brings her up. I know they're close, but then I question if guys and girls can really be friends, and all that self-doubt wasn't at all helpful when he put his hat on her head and smiled.

Fucking smiled.

And saw her tears.

I'm back at the apartment and feeling like I stole a kiss rather than gave one. I was just so angry. Mad that I was attracted to her. That it was hard to even focus while touching her... And I can only blame myself.

Shit, if anyone had seen us, it would have been game over.

I would have been in the CEO's office on my hands and knees, waiting for him to disband us before we even really debuted.

Between Haneul and me, I'm the chef, so at least I'm able to distract myself while I make the food.

I wasn't sure what the girls would like, so I went for ddukbokki, bulgogi, and since you can never go wrong with it, kimchi. Clearly, I was thinking ahead, so I grabbed the stash from the fridge. The smell of the food hits the apartment hard, and I'm suddenly ravenous.

I tell myself I'm making the food for me, when really, I just want those damn girls to eat. Haneul said that Jisoo ate a cup of fruit and then drank enough water to float her way to our apartment, only to eat half a protein bar and call it a day.

If they want to be part of our group, I want them healthy. I shudder thinking back on my trainee days. No joke, Sookie once sent me a text with a chicken meme and said he was going to end it all.

Panicked because that shit isn't a joke, I called him. He was in tears because the label said he needed to lose more weight. I was pissed and told SWT's leader, then showed up at their apartment with homemade food. I quickly realized that it was more Sookie just trying to prove himself, being stressed out, and not admitting it to anyone, including the leader or his manager.

Ugh. I disgust myself. I shove away from the stove and reach for my phone, pulling it from the charger to send Sookie a quick text.

Me: *I'm sorry. I lost my temper…again.*

Sookie responds right away.

Sookie: *Gae Sae Ggi*

Me: *Yes, I'm aware. I'm a jerk, thank you.*

Sookie: *Gae Ji Ral*

Me: *Are you practicing cursing at people? This is fun.*

His texts stop, so I try again.

Me: *Look, I have no excuse. Well, I mean I do, but…never mind. It's a long story.*

Sookie: *Soju?*

Ah, there he is. At least he still wants to drink with me.

Me: *Yeah, I can't tonight, but later. And stop cursing at me.*

The doorbell rings. I set my phone down and walk over to open it. It rings again. I pull it open and really wish I wasn't wearing an apron.

Or anything.

Ah-Ri looks adorable in her little adidas outfit. I almost forget to ask her to come in. Her eyebrows arch.

She's pretty—without makeup and with it—but something about the pink tone of her lips drives me crazy.

"Oh, sorry. Come in." I open the door wider and check out her ass in those sweats when she takes off her shoes, slipping her feet into the slippers we keep by the door for guests.

She bends over just once.

And all I can whisper under my breath is, "Sshi-Bal."

Fuck.

"What's wrong?" Ah-Ri turns around and puts her hands on her hips.

I close my eyes quickly. "I just got dust in my eyes from…outside."

I open one eye.

Ah-Ri looks behind me. "From the hallway?"

I rub my eyes and clear my throat. "Yeah, we have really dusty hallways here."

"Okayyyyy." Great, so I've made her hate me more, and now she thinks I'm a dumbass besides.

The doorbell saves me.

I turn and open the door yet again.

Jisoo stands there holding her arms in front of her as if she needs a barrier between the world and herself.

She's wearing loose black track pants, some worn-looking Nikes, and a big hoodie.

I breathe a sigh of relief, thankful that she's comfortable enough around us that she doesn't feel the need to dress up for a group dinner—or, I guess, a meeting. She sneezes the minute she opens her mouth to say hi, and I'm suddenly so thankful for her nervousness because it proves my dust theory.

She has her hair slicked back into a smooth ponytail, a pink stain on her lips, and looks petrified to talk to me.

How the hell is this going to work?

She knows me.

Has for years.

She's shorter than average and always kind of reminded me of the girl next door, that is until you put makeup and a costume on her and toss her up on stage. Then, she turns into a tiger.

It's incredible to watch.

She lost by one vote on a trainee variety show. The group that went on without her ended up disbanding two years later, but still, she's hungry for it, despite looking like a little lamb that's ready to run from the wolves.

"Hey." Ah-Ri steps around me. "It's good to finally get to hang out with you outside of practice." She bows slightly.

Jisoo's face lights up. She repeats the sentiment, takes off her shoes, slides her feet into the slippers, and walks into the apartment with Ah-Ri while I follow.

Slytherin suddenly makes an appearance around the corner. Normally, his black-and-white fur would be standing on end because of strangers.

This time, the traitor prances right after them and meows.

I nearly groan when Ah-Ri picks him up. "He's so cute!"

Jisoo looks equally entranced.

The cat gets better attention. Perfect.

I stop walking, roll my eyes, then look down at both pairs of shoes they left at the door.

I don't know why.

It bothers me how worn they are.

Jisoo's have holes, and Ah-Ri's aren't much better.

Guilt assaults me.

Mainly because I know that while Haneul and I have something to prove to the industry, even if we fail and our pride gets damaged, we still have plenty of money.

Loads of it, actually. And not just from sponsorships but because our dads are loaded.

Mine owns a tech company.

And Haneul's is a surgeon.

Haneul wanders into the room, says hi to the girls, and gives me a funny look.

"The meal is almost done," I announce while the girls awkwardly go sit on the couch. They're still talking, though, so that's good.

"What?" Haneul stops in front of me. "Why does your face look like that?"

"They need new shoes." I nod to the floor. "In fact, I bet you anything, the reason they aren't eating much is because of their daily stipend. Either eat using all the money or save up to buy a new pair of shoes."

He curses.

So much cursing in the last hour.

I shrug. "We could always just...tell them it was from the label as a thank you for signing on with the new group."

He nods. "Go distract them. I'll get their sizes and report back." He stops and hangs his head, then smirks at me. "You're going to buy them more than shoes, aren't you?"

"That wouldn't be appropriate." I lie because he knows me too well.

Yeah, they're getting more than just shoes.

I start to really pay attention as I walk over to the girls. They both have clean clothing—perfect, almost—but it's all really faded.

I awkwardly try to measure their bodies and then realize I haven't spoken a word. I'm literally just staring them down as if I've lost the ability to have a conversation.

Naturally, the dumbass assumption is here to stay, isn't it?

"So." I clap my hands.

Ah-Ri jumps in response.

Good, maybe I can scare the shit out of her a second time and look like a serial killer while doing it.

One can only hope.

I shake my head

Slytherin stares up at me like I've lost it.

If he hissed, I'd understand.

"Um." I cough into my hand. "Sorry, umm—"

"The dust again?" Ah-Ri offers. "It must have made its way from the hall all the way to the couch." She grabs a pillow and hits it as if she's imagining it on my face.

I smile and look away. "Do you guys want something to drink? Water? Soda? Soju?"

"I vote that." Jisoo pipes up. "It's our first dinner, isn't it?"

Her voice is smooth when she talks, just like when she sings. I jump to my feet a little too fast and move toward the fridge, thankful that Jisoo could feel the tension rolling off me in waves.

I grab a few small glasses and bottles.

Haneul meets me over by the couch.

Ah-Ri reaches for a bottle, jerks back, reaches again, and then gives me a look. "Can we please just be casual? Because if I have to pour for you every single time, I might slip in some arsenic."

Haneul starts coughing and hitting his chest.

I smirk. "Deserved that. And, yeah, casual it is."

I know she's referring to the fact that she's the youngest in the group. Technically, we're her seniors, but honestly, we're all equals now.

"So…" Haneul takes his first shot. "How's practice going?"

"Good," Ah-Ri answers before I have the chance to say anything. "We nailed the song already. And our choreography—"

"Is hard," I answer.

She chokes on her sip.

Haneul looks between us.

I truly can't help it. Part of me wants to break her down to get her attention, to practice with her until she's slick with sweat and she looks at me for longer than a few seconds. Maybe the whole *I'll take your hate if I can't have your love* is a real thing. Is that what I'm feeling?

I want her more than any bandmate should want someone he has to work with—especially given the circumstances.

"Should we eat?" She's still not looking at me, but I see her stare at my stupid apron. I immediately want to die and crawl into the ground, letting it swallow me whole. *Please let it be the one without the laughing cows on it.* The moment throws me off guard, and I suddenly can't remember which one I chose. I look down and then breathe a sigh of relief.

"Ryan cooked." Haneul offers this information freely and then points at me. I don't know why I'm embarrassed now, other than the fear of the cow apron. Both girls turn to me, clearly impressed. "He likes food."

"Correction, I *love* food," I say.

I get up and nearly trip when Ah-Ri moves to her feet at the same time.

"You guys go get everything ready. Jisoo and I will figure out a way to beat your asses at the next song." Haneul winks.

Ah-Ri follows me into the kitchen.

I can hear her stomach rumbling.

Our kitchen is really modern, and I'm sure she's looking around and wondering why we get to stay in this nice apartment while she's at the trainee dorms.

"So, um, plates are just over there." I point to one of the cupboards.

She grabs them in silence, just like the chopsticks and everything else we need from the kitchen. We move around each other how we dance—with barely restrained tension.

More from her than me.

Probably because of the kiss.

Again, my fault.

"Anything else?" She leans against the counter.

"Yeah." I take off my apron, hang it up, and try not to focus on the hat she's wearing that makes me feel as if Sookie's claimed her already. "I'm sorry."

Her head jerks up. "What?"

"I'm sorry I was an ass," I say through clenched teeth. "I don't know what I was thinking."

She thunks on the head with her finger. "You weren't." She sighs. "Thinking."

Am I ever thinking these days with her around?

"Right." I get the food ready. "We should eat."

"Mmm, we should." Her eyes lock on mine.

This won't end well. That's all I keep thinking as we stand there in silence until Haneul comes in with Jisoo, saying he's starving his ass off.

Ah-Ri and I don't talk for the rest of the time it takes us to eat. I steal glances at her and feel stupid that she's just carrying on with life as if we never kissed. As if we never fought.

Maybe that's why I'm mean.

I would rather have her anger. At least then she's giving me attention.

"I'll be right back." I jump up from dinner and grab my phone.

They don't have to know.

She might not ever know.

I call the store and start making arrangements.

If all I can do is give her shoes, will it be enough?

I don't know.

But nobody in our new group will have holes in their shoes.

Not if I can help it.

I ignore my dad's call twice before making more arrangements, knowing he's going to pressure me into giving up the idol life and coming to work with him to keep the whole family dynasty.

Maybe that's why Haneul and I get along so well. We both get it. We have dreams, but they don't align with our fathers'—and never have.

I just want to create.

My father wants me to go to university.

And Haneul's dad?

He wants him to pretend to love everyone to make more money.

I would rather work five part-time jobs.

I sigh and walk back down the hall, frowning and pausing when I hear hushed voices.

It's Haneul, and he's leaning toward Ah-Ri.

And she's smiling!

What the hell?

I watch and listen in.

"You're doing good," he compliments.

Ah-Ri's head snaps up. "I'm surprised you know how to say nice things to me."

He hangs his head and gets in closer. "Look, I was young and immature and terrified of having my first audition kiss with a girl in a room full of producers."

Her eyes widen. "That's why you were an ass?"

"Yeah," He laughs. "No excuse. But what's yours?"

"Tit for tat?" she offers.

"If this is going to work, we should bury the hatchet," Hanuel whispers.

"I'm still trying to get over the fact that my nemesis from when I was seventeen was an ass because he was nervous."

"Boys are stupid," he says quickly. "Just ask Ryan."

Did she just giggle?

Laugh?

Touch him?

I clench my fists as he closes in more. They're nearly chest to chest.

"I'm sorry."

He apologized? The hell? He's always insisted she was the worst thorn in his side.

She pretends as if he hasn't been the same for her for years. What world did I just get dropped into?

"Me, too," she says.

"That went better than I thought." His smile is wide. Too wide. Is he fucking flirting with her? Because I don't like this feeling in my gut. "I really am, and I should have said it sooner. I just felt like an idiot, and then our group took off and…while I know they're all excuses, I want to do better. With you." He nods. "Deal?"

He holds out his hand. She takes it, and then he pulls her closer. I swear on all that's holy if he kisses her, I'll end him.

He doesn't.

But it looks like he might want to.

Or maybe that's just me.

He steps back, winks, then walks off.

I exhale a sigh of relief. When did I start getting so possessive of her? To the point of willing to go to prison.

My heart's beating so fast I feel as if I've just been put through choreography on top of a workout after a concert.

I stumble my way down the hall and see her standing there.

I stop and stare at her. Really stare at her. Every single feeling that I've been repressing bubbles to the surface after seeing her with my best friend. After seeing him smile, and her grin back at him. It was easier to keep my feelings buried when I thought they still didn't like each other. I could easily follow suit. But the minute he confessed things to her, I lost all self-control.

I'm officially losing it.

I hang my head as I approach her.

And then I whisper, "I didn't kiss you to teach you a lesson."

Her head jerks up. "What did you say?"

The words just tumble out without my permission. I'm trying to think of something else to say that will make it better, but all I can think of is food. She needs sustenance. We all do, and I need to stop thinking about the kissing.

"Let's keep eating."

I don't repeat myself. I'm afraid to.

So, I keep walking.

Let her solve the equation. I said what I said.

She's quiet for the rest of the night.

And I don't blame her.

When Haneul suggests that we start having practices together in a few days, I decline. It has everything to do with my selfishness and nothing to do with the group.

I'm clearly off to a great start.

Chapter Eight

Ah-Ri

Practice is brutal, and after both Haneul's and Ryan's little confessions the night before, I don't really know what to expect. Especially from Ryan.

I should have known the devil would show up, and that practice would make me want to fight someone or something.

Mainly him.

The next song had some of the hardest choreography I've ever dealt with, which is saying something since I've been a trainee for a long time. I fell about a million times.

My ass will likely have bruises larger than my body by the time we're done, though I have to admit, the choreo is perfect for the fast-paced song.

"Again," Ryan says, just as out of breath as I am.

Guess the whole confession about kissing me is long gone, and we're back to being mortal enemies now.

Yay us.

I start at the top, and Ryan dances next to me. I see our perfect reflections in the mirror and hate how pretty yet sexy he is as he hits every move next to me. His hat flies off, and he doesn't even go to grab it, just keeps dancing as if his life depends on it. So, I follow suit until I trip over my feet and collide with him.

He falls back but catches me.

I grunt, slamming against his chest. "S-sorry."

"Shoelaces," he says, his lips close to mine. "You should tie them."

"Wow, good idea, thanks." I scramble off him and almost burst into tears. They're my practice shoes, and I just lost like half my shoelace on both of them.

Going home to my parents and asking for a new pair of sneakers because I've lost the laces and have holes forming at the bottom feels shameful, and I don't have enough money to buy any.

I look away from Ryan because I'm embarrassed and slowly kick off my shoes. "I dance better barefoot anyway."

Yeah, both shoes are done.

I've had them for over five years.

I have never felt more poor or stupid. I can't even afford shoes now? In front of the one guy who makes me nervous? Who kisses me? The ex-bully?

The universe isn't playing fair. It gives me my dream and then makes me pay for it in tears every single day.

I slowly put my shoes over in the corner and make my way to the middle of the dance floor.

Ryan's silent, staring at me through the mirror. I hate that he sees me now. That he sees the vulnerability.

The pain.

The struggle.

The fight.

"Okay." He nods. "Again."

We dance for the next hour. I struggle a bit because…yeah, no shoes, but I try hard, and he says nothing, which I guess is a win in my book.

Thankfully, all I have today is choreography while I learn the next song back at the dorms.

We finish our dancing, and I suddenly realize that we're debuting in a few short weeks and don't even have a name for our group.

"What? What's that look?" Ryan laughs.

I almost swat him. "We don't even have a name!"

"Sure we do." He grins. "It's MNE or Mine."

"Mine? Why Mine?" I ask.

He leans in and grins. "Because this is ours. This thing we're doing is different, but it's going to be ours. Fuck everyone else."

I smile for the first time today. "Yeah, fuck 'em."

"Anyone ever tell you how sexy you look when you curse?" he asks.

My breath hitches.

The lights suddenly go off in the dance studio.

"Power outage?" I say.

"Good timing," he replies. Leaning in, he pulls me into his arms. We're both sweaty, and I know I want him to touch me even as I want to push him away because I don't understand him.

He stares down at me. "You were a bad idea from the start."

"And you were bad from the very beginning." I lift my chin.

He lowers his head.

I go in first.

I kiss *him*.

His tongue invades my mouth the minute our lips touch. I tell myself it's the adrenaline from working out too hard or maybe just the darkness, but I know it's him. I cling to his shirt and pull it over his head.

He doesn't hesitate at all as he spins me around and presses me against the nearest wall.

Why do bad ideas always feel so good?

I moan when he starts trailing kisses down my neck. If we get caught, we're completely screwed. But I'm willing to risk everything—including my dreams—for just one more taste of him, one more flick of his tongue. His chest heaves as he deepens the kiss.

The lights flicker back on.

We break apart so fast you'd think our parents just walked in and announced we had to get married.

I wipe my mouth.

He licks his lips.

I want more.

"Sorry," I say.

"I'm not." His response is quick, and then he pulls me in for a tight hug. "You did good today. Go home and sleep."

I want to rest my head against his shoulder so badly that it physically hurts. Tears sting the backs of my eyes because...why? Why does it have to be him of all people? Why did I have to fall for him? Why am I falling?

I don't realize how much I needed the compliment until a tear falls onto his shirt. He says nothing, just holds me tightly and then tenses more when the door opens.

Shit, it's over.

Someone found us touching.

Scandal awaits.

Instead, he breathes a sigh of relief and curses.

I look up and see Sookie watching us, the look in his eyes calculating.

"Ready?" he asks in English.

"Almost," Ryan says and literally turns away from Sookie. He holds me close and then kisses my forehead before releasing me.

I have zero words.

Ryan grabs his bag and leaves me alone in the room.

I crumple to the floor and cry.

I think I know why but, really, it's because the bully in my nightmares is the same one I want to dream with.

His kisses.

I touch my mouth.

The door opens again.

Jisoo walks in with Haneul, and they both drop their bags.

They frown at me.

"Are you okay?" Haneul asks.

Why is everyone being so nice?

I nod and stand quickly. "Yeah, just a long practice."

"And we're just starting. It's not even six at night, and I want to nap," he jokes, his smile falling when I don't return it. "Are you sure you're okay?"

"Yeah." I stand. "Shaky legs, though. Enjoy this one."

"He's a masochist when it comes to choreography." Haneul laughs. "Where is Ryan anyway?"

"Out with Sookie." I smile. "I think they had plans. And since we've been here since six this morning, I'm out."

"Go relax," Haneul says.

Jisoo waves at me and then comes over to pull me in for a hug, which is random and weird until she whispers in my ear, "It's okay to like him."

I gasp and whisper back while Haneul stretches. "How did you know?"

She laughs—it's the first real laugh I've heard from her. She braces me with both hands. "How didn't *you* know? He watches you all the time."

"No." I shake my head.

"Yes." She nods hers. "Just know we're doing something different here, so if you like him and he likes you, nobody's going to be weird about it. I know it's not normal in groups, but…honestly, who cares at this point? This is our last shot. So, if you get love out of it, get it. And if we get to debut, great. Just don't get caught…"

"Ah, so easy." I laugh. "Getting caught."

"Hey, some people survive the scandal."

"Yeah, and others burn on the internet over and over again," I say. "I'll see you tomorrow?"

She nods. "We start group practice in two days. Maybe by then you'll have it all figured out."

"Or I'll still be confused as hell, kissing a guy I hate." I shrug.

She shakes her head and bursts out laughing.

"What's so funny?" Haneul asks.

"TikTok." Jisoo covers for me. "See ya."

I realize how much I really like her in that moment and leave with a smile on my face instead of tears. Then wonder what the hell Sookie and Ryan are really doing.

Chapter Nine

Ryan

I drink way too much with Sookie and somehow end up at Ah-Ri's dorm, attempting to sneak in. When I'm like, *wait, why isn't the door working right?*, I text her.

Me: *Here!*

Ah-Ri: *Did we have plans?*

Me: *Open the door.*

Minutes later, she's jerking me inside the room and locking the door as if we're about to get arrested. I bust up laughing but stop when she shoves me hard in the chest.

"What the hell are you doing, Ryan?"

"Seeing you." I put my hands into my pockets. "It felt like too long since I didn't get to."

She grabs her phone and starts texting furiously.

"Who are you texting?" I feel rage when I shouldn't. Just like I feel attraction where I shouldn't.

"Haneul," she says. "You need to get home, sober up, and…oh, yeah, not get caught!"

"Pleaseeeee." I stumble toward the small, worn couch. "It's too late for me to get caught. Besides, can't I just charm my way out of it? With this?" I smile.

She glares.

"Maybe not." My smile drops. "Just let me crash for tonight. I promise I'll keep my hands to myself, though my mouth always has other plans."

She shrieks.

Or I think she does. I'm too tired to do anything but lie down and close my eyes.

The last thing I remember is her saying, "You know you really are an asshole."

Can't argue that.

For some reason, it makes me laugh as I burrow into the cushions. Her couch smells like her—everything actually smells like her. I like it. Too much.

Because she somehow feels like the home I haven't had in a really long time.

I close my eyes.

What feels like minutes later, I jerk my eyes open to the sound of an alarm and a pounding headache.

Oh, yeah, and an angry Ah-Ri standing over me with her arms crossed.

"Is it morning?" I ask with a groan.

"How much did you drink?"

I cover my face with my hands. "Blame Sookie. He just kept going and going and going."

"And let me guess, you tried to keep up?" She laughs. "Nice try. That guy can drink anyone under the table. You should know that."

"But he's so younggggggg." I groan. "He just kept asking me about you, and then I told him we kissed."

She slaps a hand over my mouth. "WHAT?"

My answer comes out extremely muffled.

She moves her hand.

"Geez, are you trying to suffocate me?"

"Depends on what you said."

"I told him the truth." I start to sit up. "That I'm attracted to you and that I kissed you, once out of denial and anger and twice out of need."

"Are you still drunk?" She feels my forehead. "Do you have a fever?"

I slap her hands away. "No, I'm just being honest, but thanks for making me feel better."

I start to stand and stumble back.

"Wow, still drunk." She sighs. "Okay, so I guess we're going over the next song here in the dorm unless you want to take me home."

"Like takeout." I laugh. "Oh, God, maybe I am still drunk."

"Um, yeah."

"Bring the chopsticks!" I shout and then add, "I miss spicy rice cakes."

"Well, maybe I can grab your card and get all the food on the way to your place without getting us both kicked out of this label and caught."

"Onward!" I yell. "Fucking loved that movie. My sister was like my brother…"

"Okayyyyy." Ah-Ri helps me up. "Let's put a hat on you and get out of here. Your apartment had better have security so I can sneak you in."

"Basement elevator," I say, dizzy as hell. "Just walk like normal into the building, go to the basement elevator, and we can go to the penthouse."

"Or I can call Haneul."

"Or that." I yawn. "So tired."

"I know, big guy. So tired."

"Big-dick energy."

"You should nap today." She laughs. "Like for a *very* long time. And hydrate. I'll make you some Hangover Soup, all right?

"I love Hangover Soup," I say.

I remember sunglasses, a hat, and sneaking out into the bitter cold before taking a taxi back to my apartment and then getting tucked into bed with a blanket.

Then music.

I remember the music.

She's working on the wrong song, and I don't even care because I love her voice. I also smell soup. I get up and toss the blanket to the floor, then walk out to the main living space.

Ah-Ri has headphones on and keeps singing her part and taking notes. She looks up, and I swear I want to bottle that expression and keep it forever.

"Hey." She smiles. "Made you soup."

"Marry me," I grumble.

"Meh, I have better prospects." Her smile's kind.

"Probably because you make good soup." I nod. "I respect that."

"Still drunk?"

"No, but going to go kill Sookie later. Wanna join?"

"I mean, I like him, but I've always wondered if I could get away with murder."

"Well, on that terrifying note…" I laugh. "Thank you for taking care of me and making sure we didn't get caught."

She shrugs. "All in a day's work."

"You work hard," I say, walking past her. She needs to know how amazing she is, and I don't know how to even tell her without getting weird about it. I'm falling fast and hard. The last time that happened, it didn't end well.

Maybe that's my weakness, my thing: falling and then crashing to the ground, waiting for my friends to clean up the mess.

I think of Haneul and swallow a lump in my throat.

And then I think about my sister and try to replace that thought with happy things because it's just so damn depressing.

The doorbell rings, and I immediately want to rip it out of our building. Ah-Ri freezes on the couch. I shake my head. "It's fine. Just stay there."

I casually walk over to the door and open it.

My smile's so big I can't contain it.

Shit, perfect timing.

"Delivery." The guy wants my signature.

I'm still smiling when I take the big box into the room and put it on the table.

Ah-Ri pulls off her headphones. "What's this? Team uniforms?"

"Something like that." I smirk. "Open it."

She frowns and then slowly stands to look at the box. "I think I might need a knife with all this tape."

"Please." I roll my eyes and pull the box open. "You just need muscle."

"And you need humility. Guess everyone wins today."

"Cute. Now, look." I jerk my head toward the box as she slowly starts to unravel what's inside.

Two pairs of shoes for each girl.

Two athletic outfits for dance practice.

Ah-Ri's hands tremble as she grabs the Jordans and looks at them. Brand-new and not cheap, she drops one shoe.

"Sorry, it's just…" A tear slides down her cheek. "I was so"—more tears come—"I had no more practice shoes and didn't want to ask my parents. And—"

I pull her in for a hug. "It's okay."

"How did you know? I just broke those shoes yesterday."

I kiss her on the forehead. "Doesn't matter. Haneul and I just want to make sure our group looks the best. It's a totally selfish move on our part, you know."

She laughs, nods, then holds out a white Jordan with pink and black on the sides. "Yeah, this is about you then?"

"Totally."

"And the clothes?" she asks.

"Oh, we ordered in a bigger size because we fully intend to make sure you eat more food." I wink. "That okay?"

She drops the shoe.

Then hugs herself.

Then collapses onto the couch. "Nobody's ever given me gifts like this before."

"Good." I join her on the sofa. "Then I get to be the first."

She smiles. "Of so many things."

"So many," I agree with a wink. "Now, go feed me soup. I did just buy super badass shoes for you."

She bursts out laughing. "Yeah, okay, but just this once."

I pull her against me and hug her, then whisper in her ear. "Wear the shoes, and don't feel guilty. Wear the outfit. Feel beautiful and know your life will change. I promise."

"And if it doesn't?" She's still against my chest.

"Then you'll still have me."

"Don't make promises you can't keep."

"I'm not," I say simply. "I don't know if you've noticed, but I'm kind of attached to my little anti-fan right now."

"Because you won't let go."

"No," I vow. "I won't."

"Soup," she whispers. "Then songs."

"Soup first. Songs later."

"And after that?"

I hesitate, then kiss her forehead again. "We'll see."

Chapter Ten

Ah-Ri

I'm still at his apartment.

We've had soup.

Worked on the song.

And I know Jisoo and Haneul are gone, working on choreography before we start practicing together next week. Which means we're completely alone. He's sober. I'm sober and yet feeling drunk off the smiles he keeps giving me.

So, I try to focus on our schedule for the debut.

I start a countdown on my phone.

Three more weeks.

That's not a lot of time.

I'm not nervous; we're all pros at this point, and we only have to debut six songs and one music video. But, still, knowing there's only one co-ed group in existence and we'll be the second is a lot of pressure.

I stare at the shoes in the box and try not to smile. I fail. I was so embarrassed about mine, and then he just randomly ordered shoes—which means he did it before all of this, and I just didn't know.

Which also means the Tin Man has a heart.

And an amazing kissing ability.

My focus is not the best right now. If I'm being honest, it's been complete shit ever since the shoes and singing for the last few hours with Ryan.

I try to pretend like it's not a big deal and that we're just hanging out, but it feels deeper. Different.

"This song is hitting differently," he says a few hours later. "I think we need to fix some lyrics."

"Last minute?" I shriek. "I thought everything was set in stone. We literally have to perform this in the next month."

He turns and smiles at me. He's in a fresh black T-shirt and black sweats again with a backward Yankees hat. I love that he's so casual with me when we work.

It's almost sexier than if he were all dressed up, though I know what that looks like, too.

Shiny lips. Perfect contacts. Hair. Designer clothes.

Like, damn. This guy on a normal day is otherworldly, but put him in all his stuff, and it's almost hard to look at him. He's so pretty and masculine.

His hair's getting longer, already touching the nape of his neck.

Is it weird that I want to pull it?

Focus.

Focus!

"So, what's wrong with the lyrics?" I clear my throat.

"They don't feel as passionate as the dancing." He stands. "So, like this move goes like this." He does this crazy hip roll spin thing that has me nearly hypnotized. "But the words don't feel like they match." He sighs and tosses his hat onto the couch. "Then the music slows, and it just feels…" He kicks the couch. "Wrong."

I think about it and stand. "Maybe it's not the words but the choreography. Jisoo and Haneul aren't working on this one today, so maybe we fix that first."

He stills and then looks over at me, his brown eyes locking on me, making it hard to breathe. "That's a good idea."

"Okay, then." I swallow, my throat dry at the way he looks at me now. I can't explain it, so I just go with it.

This is work, right?

"We don't have a ton of space in here." I look around at the furniture.

"C'mon," he says. "We'll go to one of the spare bedrooms. There's really nothing in there since the other guys moved out."

His jaw clenches.

"Is that what happened?" I pry.

He laughs, but it sounds bitter. We walk toward a random room. "Yeah, well, we hit it pretty big and could have been bigger, but things went downhill when they decided they wanted to do their military service sooner rather than later without telling us. So, yeah, that's what happened. Then…boom, disbandment that nobody really knows about yet. I'm sure people assume, but…it sucks. It was our first group, Haneul and me. After solo projects, it just felt right, and then the guys made choices without us. One of them had a few acting projects already and wanted to stop touring."

I touch his shoulder. "I'm sorry."

"I was, too. And now I'm thinking maybe it was for the best." He's looking right at me. My stomach does somersaults as he opens the door to the empty room.

There's a bed, a desk, and that's it. The room is pretty sparse, giving us enough space to dance, though it's still intimate.

He grabs his phone, turns on the song, and sets it on the desk. "So, let's figure this out."

It feels too intimate, but I listen to the song.

When it gets slower, we need to make it more…personal.

I walk up to Ryan and wrap my arms around him. "Maybe we make it more like a ballet."

"A ballet?" he asks.

I nod. "What if you lift me, put me down, and dance with me like it's a dream? Like we're in an actual dream during this sequence. Haneul can do the same with Jisoo. And then we'll come together with the last part of the song and look up since it mentions clouds, and then fall together on the ground staring at them. We can use our arms to do some choreography that matches, and then we just…fall asleep."

He says nothing for a while.

The song plays on repeat.

Suddenly, I'm taken on a journey as Ryan lightly pushes me back with his fingers. They run down my face, my neck. He turns me around and then lifts me up and over his shoulders, dropping me, spinning me.

We dance around each other, and it feels so emotional that I start to cry as I think about the lyrics, being in the clouds, in love, wanting something so badly.

He pulls me against him as the lonely lyrics sound.

I dance around him.

It's as if we were born to dance together.

I spin again, and he lifts me and turns us both as I slide down his body. And then we're apart, and I don't want to be.

I want him.

I run at him as he lifts me.

I fall against him, and we crumple to the floor as if we're looking up at the stars. He points up. I smile and point, as well. We turn toward each other and smile, and then I'm pulled into him.

And that's where I stay.

His lips lower.

So close.

The door opens and closes.

We don't move.

The door to the room opens.

"Ummmm?" Jisoo says. "Should I leave you two?"

"We fixed it," Ryan says. "The choreography."

"It's perfection." I nod.

"Thanks to you," he says. "Get Haneul. We have work to do."

We work on the choreography for the next two hours. Both Haneul and Jisoo are obsessed with it, and we soon all have it down.

"I think this is our first song," Ryan says after we order food. "It hits differently. I feel it."

Jisoo nods. "I did, too."

Haneul looks at all of us. "Well, we're already taking a risk with a co-ed group. Let's do it."

We all nod in agreement and then eat until Haneul's phone goes off.

It's actually the first time in a long time that I don't start counting the calories before putting the food into my mouth and it feels good. I have Ryan to thank for that; for making me feel braver, and beautiful. For kissing me and feeding me, two things I never knew I needed.

Frowning, he looks down at it. "It's our manager."

I've yet to meet him; not that I care since we aren't really doing any shows or anything yet.

Haneul answers it, and I can see his skin visibly pale as he listens.

When he's done, he puts the phone down and rasps. "Seems SWT might have a surprise release coming up or something. If we want to release our first single, we probably need to do it in the next week or wait for two months."

I jump to my feet. "What? Why?"

"Because," Ryan says next to me, "when SWT releases or does anything, it saturates the market. Not just with their music but backlist music and merch, too. We need to be seen, so…"

"Shit," Jisoo cusses.

We all look at her.

She shrugs. "What? It's shit. We all know it. And it sucks."

"We'll do the song," I say. "The one we just did. We'll do that one first. We can do a teaser MV, right? How long does that take?"

Ryan runs his hands down his face. "We have the concept already, but we have to get production ready and—"

"I can do it," Jisoo suddenly says. "My mom's dating CEO Siu. I bet I can get them to swing it this week. I'll ask."

Stunned stupid, I just stare at her. "Your mom is dating the CEO of our label?"

She frowns. "I didn't think it was necessary to share."

Haneul bites back a curse while Ryan laughs. "Anyone want soju?"

"Cheers." I join him in laughter. "Looks like we're doing a teaser MV this week. No pressure. Who the hell is even going to edit that?"

"Me," Haneul says. "I'm good. As long as we have the manpower to get a teaser and MV done, I can edit and direct the entire thing."

It's not just risky; it's unheard of. I mean, other than Stray Kids and a handful of other groups.

Then again, look at them now. Stray Kids just hit number one on the US billboard charts for their latest album, so maybe this is the right move to make.

So, I just nod my head and agree.

And when I go to bed later that night…

I dream of dancing with the guy who used to taunt my nightmares, only to enter into my dreams.

Chapter Eleven

Ryan

Two Days Later

Jisoo was actually able to pull it off. We're doing the dream sequence scene on set for a teaser, and while we've been given so much opportunity, the team at FS has been very clear that if we fail in this, we're done.

No pressure.

CEO Siu even comes to our rehearsal before the teaser.

All of us are in chains.

The girls are in these angelic fairy costumes, and we look like fallen angels with dark purple wings. All of us are fighting the chains, moving back and forth as we move in sync towards one another.

We break free and then find our other halves, giving so much more meaning to the name I put in Ah-Ri's phone weeks ago. The fallen angel, coming to find her. Coming home to the one girl he was supposed to be with all along but was too afraid to take. The minute we touch hands, the stage lights are supposed to brighten, and then we start to dance.

The girls look like haunted ballerinas, and we look like demons ready to possess them until we start to touch and dance with them. Slowly, the red contacts are removed from our eyes, the crazy hair, and we begin to look more human.

At the end, it's just us dancing with them.

And me trying so hard not to fall even further into this obsession with Ah-Ri.

I lean in as if I'm going to kiss her, then spin her around, lie down on the fake grass with her, and point at the sky.

The other two lie down next to us.

When we finish the teaser and music video, I hear clapping.

Actual clapping.

I look up.

The CEO of the entire label is clapping for us. He nods his head at me and winks. "I hope this works. I really do."

"Me, too." I feel like puking. "Me, too."

It takes me a minute to get out of hair and makeup. By then, I'm exhausted, and everyone else has decided to go their separate ways to take a nap.

Everyone but Ah-Ri.

I follow her out of the building and watch her get into the van that will take her back to the trainee dorms, even though I know they're close.

I follow.

Like a creeper.

She gets out of the van and goes into the dorms. I pull my baseball hat down, follow her, and then knock on her door.

She opens it, frowning.

I push her back in.

She throws off my hat. "You scared me to death!"

"Sorry," I say. "I was just…wanting some…ramyeon."

"And I'm the chef now?" She rolls her eyes and closes the door. "And no ramyeon. You may as well ask for Netflix and chill."

"Same thing?" I mean, it sort of is, and my body's completely on board with it after today. I would love to Netflix and chill or eat *ramyeon.* God, she's so pretty it hurts.

"Same thing." She nods. "Now, if you'll excuse me, I need a nap."

I yawn behind my hand. "Yeah. Me, too."

"No." She points a finger at me. "You're already confusing enough and—"

"Me?" I point at myself. "Confusing? I just didn't want to go all the way home. You're closer."

She sighs and looks up at the ceiling in annoyance. "Fine. Couch. Go. No ramyeon."

"Deal." I just want to be close to her, so I go to her couch and lie down as if I'm really tired, even though just seeing her has adrenaline coursing through my system.

She goes into her bedroom. When she comes out to get water, I see she's changed her clothes. She's in black sweatpants and a white tank top now. The lights are off in the apartment as she grabs a water bottle from the fridge and returns to her room. I stare at her, even though I know I shouldn't.

The couch is comfortable, and still smells like her. It's this weird addiction I didn't realize I wanted or needed as I toss and turn with the blanket I grabbed.

Then I finally open the door to her room and wander in.

"What could you possibly want?" she asks.

"A small spoon," I answer.

"Like I said, NO ramyeon!"

"No, I mean like this sort of spoon." I crawl onto the bed, fully ready for her to knee me in the balls or yell at me.

Instead, she relaxes against me and mumbles, "This means nothing, even if I'm the small spoon."

"It means nothing even if I'm the big spoon."

She huffs.

And falls asleep.

The last thing I remember is her reaching for my hand.

When I wake an hour later, she's sprawled on me, her legs tangled with mine. I don't have the heart to move, even though I'm starving. She sighs and nudges my neck with her chin.

It's heaven.

Just like our song.

I hold her tightly.

And *then* I get kneed in the balls.

"Son of a bitch!" I yell.

"Oh, no!" Ah-Ri pulls away from me. "I'm so sorry! I had a nightmare."

"About my dick?" I yell.

She bursts out laughing and says, "You know, tiny things are scary."

"Take it back." I groan, still in pain but able to flip her onto her back as she laughs.

"Never!" Ah-Ri announces.

I start to tickle her sides.

She lifts her leg. "Don't you dare."

Her stomach growls.

Mine is getting ready to do the same.

I want to kiss her, but food first. I pull away. "Want me to order dinner?"

"You paying?"

"Do I get something for paying?" I ask.

She holds up her hand.

I punch it with my fist and then rest my palm against hers. "Worth it."

Her breath hitches.

I don't want to ruin the moment, so I leave the room and grab my phone, my hands trembling.

Our palms kissed again.

I'm such a nerd.

But I smile the entire time I look for some good places to eat.

Later that night, when we're sitting across from each other, I realize it's still too far.

It will always be too far if I'm away from her.

We decide on pizza, and as she eats in front of me, I don't think I've ever seen a girl throw back so many slices in my entire life. It's attractive as hell, and I find myself watching while she chomps down. I'm so proud of her for eating that I can't stop smiling.

"You have sauce, right there." I point to her chin and then rub the sauce off with my thumb.

She blushes, swallows, and looks away. "Sorry. I was starving."

"Same." I'm not talking about the pizza. I drop my slice and continue to stare. Something about her inspires me and makes me want more than I'm allowed to have. How did this even happen?

"I like it when you eat," I whisper.

She blushes and looks down. "I feel stronger now."

"You were always strong."

I think of raw beauty, the kind you struggle to explain with just one word. She's fierce. Powerful. She's like a thorn on a rose that you're afraid to touch but need to feel in order for the pain to cleanse you.

She's everything.

And I'm afraid to say anything. So, I sit and watch like an idiot while she eats, while I eat, while we both act like there isn't this weird tension in the room because of me. Because of us.

So much is at stake, and I feel sick to my stomach.

I may even puke up the pizza I ate.

So much hinges on this.

Not just my career but also Haneul's and the girls'. We have one shot, one chance. Shit, we're like the Avengers at this point because I know how brutal things can get if we fail, and it's not like our label is super behind us, even though our CEO loved the performance. If the fans hate it, the label will cut us.

This is called our one shot.

A chance.

Because they trust Haneul and me, but…

Shit.

My stomach makes a noise, though not because I'm hungry. I'm just freaking the fuck out over all the pressure on us.

"Be right back." I stand and run to the bathroom. I don't puke, but I do stand there and think about all the groups that have made it despite the circumstances and in spite of even their labels being against them.

Weirdly enough, I keep going. If Stray Kids made it doing things on their terms, so can we.

But…

Despite their hella hard work, it kind of feels like a lottery.

One we could lose.

"Hey," Ah-Ri sounds through the bathroom door. "You okay?"

"Totally fine," I lie. It seems I always lie to her these days. "Just…thinking."

"Yeah, I totally do that for hours in the bathroom, too."

I laugh despite the stress. "I'll be out soon."

"Should I be worried?"

"Totally. Let's burn the building."

"I'll grab the matches," she kids.

And I love her for it. I love that she's making it so I'm not so stressed. So I'm smiling rather than frowning and wondering if the world really will burn.

"Oh yeah?"

"I'm a good partner in crime."

"And to think I didn't realize I needed one of those until now," I say.

The door opens, and I see her poke her head in. Fuck, she's pretty.

And I hate how pretty she is because it's so damn distracting when I need to focus.

"Good." She walks in, and the door clicks shut.

It feels like one of those moments.

The ones where you're like, *oh, shit, this might actually be it, and I might never come back from this.* But I don't even care anymore because…

Her.

So, I wait.

I wait for her to approach me.

And she does.

I'm still, completely unable to move but fully aware of her beautiful features, her dark hair, eyes, and the shy smile she tries to hide.

My heart hammers against my chest.

My emotions are all over the place. I try to stay calm.

And then she touches me. Just a soft brush of her fingertips against my mouth as if she's trying to figure out why we have this connection, why we both have this tension, this feeling.

I wait.

I don't want to, but I do.

She leans in and brushes a kiss across my mouth. "This is a bad idea, isn't it?"

"It was a bad idea the second I asked myself what you tasted like," I say.

She pulls away. "When was that?"

"The first argument we had," I confess. "The one where you basically told me you would taste bitter then so sweet I would probably die from it. The first time you opened that pretty damn mouth. Then. It was then."

She presses her lips to mine so hard that I almost stumble backward, and I know I should stop her.

But I don't.

Because this is what I want.

What I need.

Her.

I grab her sweatshirt and pull it over her head, surprised that she lets me, and then I'm suddenly backed against the counter, pulling her with me, my hands with a mind of their own as clothes start to fall.

My phone rings in my pocket. So does hers. I want to ignore it but know that something's clearly wrong if it's not stopping. With a curse, I pull away from Ah-Ri and look down at my screen. She's already on hers.

"Jisoo texted," she says. "Something about an emergency meeting."

Dread fills my body as I answer my phone. "Yeah?"

It's Haneul.

He's already called twice.

"Look," he says, "I just got some more information. SWT *is* dropping a song early, like literally when we were supposed to release our mini-album. I guess they decided to surprise their fans as a thank you after the whole scandal with Lucas and that one fan who turned out to be setting him up in order to ruin his career. Marketing felt like it was great timing, and the buildup has been so good they went along with it."

"Of course, they are." My chest heaves. I know they don't plan this shit, and I know that it's more about timing than anything. They aren't trying to screw us, but it feels like it right now. It really does. We were already low on time. But now? Now, it's like…a clusterfuck of stress.

Ah-Ri looks at her phone. "Of course, they are. Why are we even trying? Our teaser and MV likely won't even be enough."

"Hey, this isn't over. None of this." I press a finger to her lips. "Promise me that we'll finish what we started tonight." I hold the phone away and wait for her to answer me.

She grins. "Guess you'll just have to see."

"No." I hold her tighter. "I don't think I can handle the stress, especially now. Promise me."

Her eyes soften as I hear Haneul talking through the phone. But for some reason, this seems just as important. "I promise." Her lips feel soft against my finger. "That we'll talk. Is that good enough?"

"No." I'm gruff as I pull away. "But it's all I'll get, isn't it?"

"Yeah."

"Okay." I nod.

"Okay." Her lips are swollen. I did that.

Pride wells up in me as we walk out of the bathroom and into the living room. I hop back on the phone and put it on speaker. I'm on cloud nine until Haneul continues talking.

"So, as I mentioned, SWT is releasing their single the same week we were going to drop the mini-album. We either fix our release date, or we just take our chances going up against them on the same day."

I hang my head and then look up. "We can't compete; you know that. We talked about that before when we decided to do the teaser.

They're like the next BTS."

"Yeah," Haneul says. "I'm very aware of how popular they are."

"So, we release earlier," Ah-Ri says. "And we kill it."

I know what this means.

Sleepless nights.

Stress.

More stress.

Oh, yeah, and stress.

I look at her, needing more direction than *oh, yeah, let's just do this and kill it.* This means we'll have no lives until we wrap everything.

"It's going to be brutal," she finally says and then reaches for my hand. "We have no choice. We have to make this work."

"Okay." I sigh. "So, even though it'll be weird…we ask permission to live together or at least in the same building…as a group. All of us. So we can practice."

"Is that smart?" Haneul asks on the phone. "If fans find out—I don't know, man. We can always ask or we can just bust our asses in the training rooms."

I look at Ah-Ri, knowing it's not smart at all. Still, I ask, "Do we have any other choice? I feel like we're running out of options."

"No," Haneul says. "It's this or nothing."

"All right." I sigh. "Call the label and see what we can do. If anything. Maybe the girls just come over and practice with us in the apartment when we can't use the practice rooms. We need to get to work."

"I'll get Jisoo on the phone, too," Ah-Ri says. "It looks like sleep will be a thing of the past now, huh?"

"I'm headed to the practice room. You guys in?" Haneul says through the phone.

I want to say no, but he's right; we need more practice, which means evenings and shit—just all of it.

"Yeah," I say. "We'll meet you guys there."

"We can do this," Haneul says.

I want to say: *"But can we?"*

Instead, I just agree.

Things are about to get way more complicated.

Chapter Twelve

Ah-Ri

It's late, and I'm confused. I still taste him on my lips, and now we're all in the practice room at the label, trying to figure out what to do with our next four songs and pull off this seemingly impossible feat.

Recording them isn't going to be the issue.

No, the problem will be the choreography for our Showcase. In the States, you release your single or album and see how things go. You don't have the same Showcase that we do in Korea. It's so much pressure that it makes me want to crawl under the covers of my bed when I think about it.

Our Showcase will be everything.

It's our reveal to the world.

Things must be perfect.

Not only that, but we'll have variety shows and other live performances to follow, so we can't exactly be out of sync, even a little bit.

And all of this has to happen now in record time.

Hours later, as sweat pours down my face, I check my phone.

It's two in the morning, and we need to be at the studio at eight a.m. I take another drink of water, and Jisoo passes me a protein bar.

Thankful, I scarf it down and stare at myself in the mirror again.

"This choreography is harder," Jisoo says almost to herself. "It feels intense. Less fluid."

"Yeah," I agree. "It's almost…angry."

The guys are quiet.

Finally, Ryan speaks up. "My sister wrote it."

"The song?" I ask.

"Yeah." He doesn't look at me in the mirror, he just stares down at his feet. "She wrote it before she died."

"Was she angry?" Jisoo asks.

I shoot her a look.

"What?" She shrugs. "It's a powerful song, but it *is* angry."

"We wrote it together," Ryan says, seeming lost as he clears his throat. "My parents weren't always there for us. So, yeah, we wrote an angry song. I never thought it would release, but after her...after she—" He runs his hands through his hair.

"Hey, let's just focus on the dancing for now," Haneul says.

We ignore the tension, which seems to be a theme with all of us now, and I practice every dance sequence like my life depends on it. Haneul moves toward me. We're supposed to look like we're about to kiss and then are each pulled away.

He smiles at me each time we get close, and for some reason, Ryan pulls me back harder and harder from him until I'm convinced I'll fall to the floor.

"Hey," I say for the tenth time. "You don't have to jerk me away so hard."

He gulps. "Sorry." His gaze falls to Haneul. "I just wanted to make it believable."

"Yeah, well, I believe it." I shake it off. "Just trust me."

I swear that phrase hangs between us.

Trust me.

Trust us.

Trust what, though?

This weird friendship that has crossed basically every boundary ever? How do you even navigate something like that? Especially since it's not fair to our other two members, who are just trying to survive this debut.

We practice for one more hour. By the time we're done, everyone's exhausted, starving, and ready for bed.

Jisoo and Haneul leave first. I follow, not even bothering to talk to Ryan as I walk to the dorms. While it would have been convenient to live together so we could eat, sleep, and breathe the same sweaty practice air—the label said it might cause too much scandal before our debut.

Ryan's silent as he walks next to me.

I don't argue when he comes into my place and shuts the door. Just like I don't argue when he locks it and crawls into bed next to me after we both separately shower from all our hard work.

We don't discuss the lines we're continuing to cross, and I wonder how I fell for him so fast. Then, I wake up to find him holding me close.

I'm the small spoon again.

I hate that it makes me smile to wake up in his arms when I know it can only end in heartbreak.

We're in the same group. How can we ever make this work?

I don't know. But I pretend to sleep as he kisses my forehead. When the alarm from my phone sounds again, he curses, gets up, and says, "Pray you have coffee."

"Red Bull," I grumble.

"Even better." He looks like a god as he walks around my room in nothing but black boxer briefs. He puts on his white shirt from the night before and then turns and looks at me. "One day, or maybe one night…"

"Is that a threat? Or are you just too tired to finish your thoughts?" I tease.

His eyes rake down my body. "It's a promise."

He walks out of my room.

And I believe him.

I believe it's a promise, even when it feels like a threat. There is no way this will end with us parting as best friends. If it does end.

No way.

We've both already allowed ourselves to think past that. And now, we're going to be damned because of it if it ends badly or if anyone finds out.

Nobody can know.

We'll live a life of constant secrets.

So why does it still sound like a good idea when I lie back against the pillow and think about how he held me?

I justify it all.

And then I get up and go into the kitchen, wrapping my arms around his body.

He stills.

Hangs his head.

"Bad idea," he whispers.

"The worst," I agree.

He grips my wrists as if he's going to push me away, then clenches them tighter. "We'll either regret it all or—"

"Die of happiness?"

He laughs. I love the way it feels against my body. "Yeah, that." He looks over his shoulder. "You ready for today?"

"No. You?"

He shakes his head. "Not enough caffeine. But we have to make this work. I can't…" He stops himself and then sighs. "I have nothing after this. My sister was my best friend, my everything. My dad resents that I stayed in the industry after she—" His voice hitches. "After she lost her life to suicide."

My heart pounds in my chest. "I'm so sorry."

"Yeah. My family has money. They kept most of it private." Sadness fills his voice. So much that I want to take it away from him—or maybe just carry it for him. "They said it was an accident. She fell from a bridge. She was a gymnast before trying to become an idol. She would never have lost her balance."

"She…" I lick my lips. "She jumped?"

He nods. "She was depressed, had so many horrible comments about the first drama she acted in. Then her single didn't do well, and she just…lost it. Decided that being in Heaven was better than being in Hell."

A tear slides down my cheek. "I'm sorry. I had no idea…"

"It's not okay. I'm not going to say it's okay because I live with it every day." He turns in my arms. "Anyway, it's one of the reasons I want to make it. Because she never did. It was her dream, and this is our last shot. She always talked about doing a co-ed group and how badass it would be. I need to do it for her. For us. For her memory."

I grab his hand. "Then we will."

"We will," he agrees. "Or we'll get laughed out of the label. But, yeah, we'll try."

"It's all we can do," I say. "And while we've never been best friends…"

He laughs.

"Seriously." I release his hand and smack him in the chest. "I'll try my hardest to do her proud."

His eyes well with tears. "You have no idea how much that means."

He kisses my hand, and I wonder if I'm even worthy of being in this group. But I have no time to feel sorry for myself as we go to practice and sweat our asses off.

Days.

We have days to become perfect.

It's our last chance.

And I have to remember that Ryan's sister didn't have one, so I need to make it work for all of us.

And for her.

Chapter Thirteen

Ryan

Practice is brutal.

My dad's been calling more than usual lately.

I know that's not a good sign.

I finally call him back during my break and wait for him to yell at me. Instead, he's quiet, which is almost scarier than his loud voice.

"You need to come home," he says. "It's gone on long enough."

I roll my eyes. "Dad, I'm making money, I'm doing good, we're just in this new group and—"

"Your mom's worried. I'm worried. You've been on your own. You haven't even visited your sister's—"

"Dad." Tears well in my eyes. "I'm not ready for that."

There will never be a day when I *will* be ready for that. Not now. Not ever. It hurts too much. I press a hand to my chest and tell myself to breathe.

"You're not mourning."

"I mourn every fucking day!" I yell and then feel like shit because I know he is, too. "Just give me some more time."

"You've had time."

"This was her dream," I snap, knowing that I have no right to yell at him like that and hating that the anger and grief swirl together so harshly that I can't tell what I even feel anymore. "Let me make her dream come true, even if she's sleeping. Let me make her dreams come true."

"Son," he rasps. "Don't you know? She already had her dream come true. She had you. Her best friend. Her older brother. There is no doubt in my mind that she doesn't already know the battles you would fight for her, the things you would achieve in her memory. But don't let it take over your entire life. Years later, you'll miss the time spent on things like this when it could have been with family."

I know he's right, but still, it's also my dream. It's ours. It's what we shared. And while I miss my parents, I can't give up. Not yet. "I need to do this."

He's even more quiet. "Then I hope you know what you're doing and what you're sacrificing to make it happen."

A relationship with my parents? Family? Everything.

I know that.

But I can't stop.

She wanted this.

And so do I.

I can still see her smile as she danced. See the way she twirled and asked if she looked stupid or pretty.

She was beautiful. Her laugh haunts me when I'm trying to sleep. Everything about her haunts me.

"Do you think I'll make it?" she asks.

I smile and reach for her hand. Her skin is so smooth. "You'll make everyone jealous with how pretty you are, how talented. So, yes, you'll make it."

Her gaze falls. "It's a lot of pressure. Just yesterday, this girl was talking about how she went three days without eating. Her roommate finally gave her half a banana because she was worried."

There is always a dark side.

I stare her down. "Don't starve yourself. Don't be like them. Eat your food, dance, work hard, be healthy. You're perfect the way you are."

"Not to them." She looks away.

I know she's talking about the keyboard warriors online. "Don't worry about them. Just worry about you."

"I hope I can be strong like you one day." She winks.

"You already are."

She laughs. "Sureeeeee. Okay, from the top again. I have to get this eight-count right."

I play the song again and then again.

She perfects it.

And when she finally debuts, she looks like an angel—until she starts reading the comments on her Instagram and TikTok accounts.

Until she starts believing the lies people who don't even know her tell.

I dance like shit the rest of practice and refuse to talk to anyone when we take another break.

Haneul is in the hallway somewhere, and Jisoo is slumped against the floor, saying she needs at least a ten-minute nap if she's going to be able to function.

And Ah-Ri...

I frown.

Where the hell is Ah-Ri?

I look around the studio and wonder how I can be so out of it that a person can just disappear in front of me.

I leave, walk down the hall, and then stumble when I see Haneul almost pressing himself against Ah-Ri. They're in a corner.

She's looking up at him, smiling.

And he's staring down at her like it's more than friendship, even though I know it's my own insecurity crashing through me.

It's like déjà vu.

What the hell?

He pushes a piece of hair from her face, and I immediately want to murder him. What's he doing? He knows how I feel—or I guess he should know or assume or...shit. Have I even told him how deep everything goes now? Am I reading too much into this? Is it just a friendly interaction?

"Hey," I bark like I'm losing it. "We should probably get back in there."

"Oh, yeah." Haneul gives me a funny look and then shrugs and walks off, leaving Ah-Ri standing there staring at me.

I nearly growl as I back her against the wall.

The door to the practice room shuts.

I stare her down. "What was that?"

She laughs and then covers her mouth. "Oh, you're serious?"

"Dead. Serious." I press my hand against the wall by her head.

Her breath hitches.

And I do it.

I kiss her, this time not caring who sees, even if it's Haneul or Jisoo, even if it's the CEO, even if I get into trouble. Because I can't stop from feeling when I'm around her. It's not some need to mark my territory—

it's my need to make her mine and make sure she knows that I'm not going to take the easy way out this time. I'm going to choose to love her, to show her as much as I can, even though I'm risking everything.

Our mouths meet in a frenzy that has my entire body exploding as if I've just been set on fire. I don't ever want to go back. I'll taste her forever. I'll die this way.

With a smile on my face.

She moans against my mouth.

"Hey. Um, guys." Jisoo's voice sounds as we break apart. "We should probably do more practicing, less kissing."

I don't even know what to say.

Until Jisoo bursts out laughing and mumbles, "Knew it."

I wipe my mouth and pry myself away from Ah-Ri. "Sorry."

She elbows me. "Don't be. I'm not."

Touché.

God, I want to chase her down the hall and tackle her to the floor. Instead, I get to go sweat with everyone else when I'd really rather fucking sweat with her in my arms.

It feels like years until we're done with practice and back at our apartment, with both girls exhausted and starving. We order more takeout.

"Look," Jisoo says through bites. "If we just fix the lyrics on this one, I think we'll be good."

It's one of my favorites of the songs we have, and I think the concept could be really exciting.

Haneul looks at her chicken scratch. "Actually, that works. It sounds more powerful if we repeat it."

"Yup." Jisoo pats herself on the back.

"So, what's your story?" I ask. "How long have you been training?"

Jisoo looks away and swallows her last bite. "Four years. I, um, I just don't want to give up."

"Nobody does," Ah-Ri says. "It's mainly stubbornness, sadness, and starvation at this point."

Haneul laughs. "This is what I want to know. Besides the things we've already discussed, why did you always hate us so much, Ah-Ri? I mean, seriously."

"Good-looking boys," Jisoo answers for her, "are always easy to hate because it seems like they have it easy. So…yeah."

"Plus," Ah-Ri adds, "no offense, but both of you are super-rich. It's aggravating. I mean, you don't have to work hard, and could have easily just followed in your fathers' footsteps. It's both annoying and admirable."

"We choose to," Haneul says quickly. "Which still means hard work and doing what we love, despite all the hate we get from our families for it."

I can tell Ah-Ri feels guilty. Her expression falls. "That's true."

I nudge her. "No hard feelings."

"None." Haneul reaches for her hand.

I literally want to chop his off. Instead, I cough and look back at my food while Jisoo rolls her eyes and laughs. "Nice."

I ignore her and look down at my phone. "We have a few more days to perfect this. We should probably practice tomorrow again at seven or eight, then pray we don't suck."

"Sleep." Haneul gets up. "I'm gonna go get right on that. See you guys in the morning bright and early. Don't stay up too late."

"Never." Jisoo looks between Ah-Ri and me, her smile less shy. She gets up and yawns. "I'll just be on my way."

"Yeah, same." Ah-Ri stands.

She's clearly walking slower.

The door opens, and Jisoo leaves.

When it clicks shut, I swear I hear the entire room buzz with tension. I grab Ah-Ri from behind and back her against the wall, my mouth on hers before she can protest. The sound of Haneul in the bathroom has us moving down the hall.

And then it's my room.

And it's us.

I slam the door shut.

"Hey, man." Haneul's voice sounds. I gently cup my hand over Ah-Ri's mouth, feeling her full lips against my palm. "I just wanted you to know, I appreciate you. I know it's been a rough few years with your sister and with us trying to make this work."

Ah-Ri's eyes widen. I can't tell if it's fear of getting caught or curiosity over what happened in those years, but I need to get him away from the room so I can be with her.

I don't think I realized how much I've been missing.

Not until her.

Maybe that was my sister's last gift. An angel. One I can't escape and don't want to. One who's willing to look at me like she wants to simultaneously strangle and kiss me.

My sister always said that I needed someone who could put up with my shit one minute and then kiss me the next.

I clear my throat. "Thanks, man. I appreciate it."

"I'm here for you," he says. "I mean, if you want to talk right now, we can talk or something. I don't know. Shit—"

"NO!" I yell. "I mean…I'm good, just super tired. So, yeah, let's talk tomorrow."

He's quiet for a minute. "Are you sure? You don't want to talk? I can come right in and—"

"NOPE!" I say again, too loudly. "I just…I'm naked!"

"You're already naked? Is that like a line we can't cross as dudes or something? Because I've already seen your dick, I'm not impressed."

"SHUT THE FUCK UP. IT'S IMPRESSIVE!" My voice actually cracks. I want to die.

"Why are you yelling?" He laughs. "I'm just saying, dick is dick."

"But my dick is big-dick energy!" I say. "Right?"

Ah-Ri's eyes close, and she starts laughing against my hand.

I'm officially murdering my best friend.

"Errr, okay. I mean, I didn't look that close. Sometimes small things are hard to see without binoculars, so…sorry."

"BINOCULARS?" Dead. He's so dead.

Is he doing this on purpose?

Wait, does he *know* she's in here?

Ah-Ri starts laughing against my hand even harder.

Cool, so both of them are dead.

I glare at her.

Her chest heaves from laughter.

What the hell is wrong with the universe? I mean, how does a guy even get it up with two people mocking his size?

"*Stop laughing,*" I mouth with a glare.

She looks down, and then her fingers toy with my sweatpants. "*Tiny?*" Her mouth moves against my palm with the word.

"I will murder him," I say through clenched teeth. "Hope you can bail me out of prison."

"What was that?" Haneul asks.

"Nothing! Just talking to my tiny dick!" I yell.

He snorts out a laugh. "Cool, all right, see you in the morning, TD."

"TD?" I ask.

"Tiny Dick." He laughs harder. "Wow, this is so great. Oh, and good night, Ah-Ri! It's been fun!"

She freezes and then shoves against me.

I stumble, then still. The looks in our eyes mirror the same horror.

"You guys are the worst at sneaking around," Haneul says. "Just don't get caught by the label, all right? Right. Good talk. 'Night!"

Ah-Ri and I look at each other like: *Is this okay? Are we fine now that he knows?*—as if he's our dad or something.

I don't know who moves first, but Ah-Ri is suddenly in my arms, and I'm spinning her toward the bed and praying to the universe that I have condoms because I need her, I want her, and her body sliding against mine is pretty much torture at this point.

Again, good idea since we're in the same group? Probably not.

But I can't stop.

I don't want to.

Her brown eyes sweep up and down my body and then lock onto mine. "Will we come back from this?"

"If it doesn't work?" I say. "No. We won't."

"So." She steps back. "Let's practice then."

"What?" I'm confused as hell, and my body has no clue how to cool down.

"Practice." She presses a kiss against my lips. "We have another music video to film, another song to do, so let's just pretend. For now, we pretend."

"Pretend?"

"As if we're actors." She sounds so convincing. "This is the role we play."

I let her slide away from me. She grabs her phone and puts on the next song on our mini-album.

It's a sexier one that we struggled to find the right concept for.

She presses play.

When she starts to dance, I think, *I will always look back on this moment.* This is where I lost myself.

To her.

To the music.

To us.

She throws her head back and spins, then falls to the floor and rests against it, lifting her hips. My mouth goes dry as she beckons me closer with her fingers, then spins to her stomach and arches her back.

I die.

I swear I see my soul leave my body as I watch hers roll against the floor, and then she's facing me again and jumping to her feet. "I don't need you."

The lyrics blast me.

"Don't need you." She repeats in her angelic voice and turns on her heel, then bends over and starts dancing.

It's not real.

But it is.

I grab her from behind and spin her in my arms. We start dancing, our hands touching as we pull apart.

"Don't need you," I sing back. "But want you, want you, want you."

She twirls, and then her mouth is on mine.

And I have zero control left as I lift her into my arms.

We're spinning and then falling against the floor again. "You're mine."

She looks up at me. "And if it all goes bad?"

"Then we burn together," I say.

She nods. "I like that ending."

"Sometimes, the best endings are the sad ones," I whisper, nipping her lower lip and sucking it until I can't take it anymore and need more of her mouth. She responds instantly, arching into me as I pull my shirt over my head.

I reach for hers, but she almost has it off.

Somehow, I'm already kicking my sweats down.

I'm so hard it hurts.

She moans my name.

I whisper hers.

Her shoes are gone, her shirt. My fingertips dip into her underwear, and I freeze, wondering if she's going to stop me, but her hipbones brush against my knuckles. How can something so simple feel so good?

"Fuck." I grip the side of her black panties and tug them down as she helps me, moving her legs, her hips. Shit, I won't survive this.

Her lips part, and she takes more of my mouth, my tongue. I plunder,

I consume, and I have zero regrets as we deepen our kisses and go past the point of no return.

I kick off the rest of my clothes, pushing her onto the bed, and then it's just us, feverish skin pressed together, touching, feeling. She reaches for my dick, and I push her away. I won't last if her fingers grip me. I want it more than anything, but I know my limits, and she's pushing them hard.

"One minute," I whisper against her mouth and reach for a condom in my nightstand, thankful I don't have to crawl over to grab it. It's been a while. Okay, it's been a super long time. My fingers shake as I tear into the wrapper, then slide the condom onto myself. "This okay?"

She nods her head, her pretty, dark hair sliding against her face as she licks her pink lips like she can still taste me and is coming back for seconds. "I just want you."

"Thought you hated me," I tease, trying to buy time before this is all over.

"Hate. Love. Same thing." She arches her back. "I need—"

"Me," I whisper against her mouth. "Remember, we're just rehearsing."

She laughs. "Sure, rehearsing. Right."

"Makes it less terrifying that we're possibly ruining our lives and maybe the group."

"No matter what," she says, "the group stays together."

I respect her even more for saying that. "No matter what."

My tip's close to her entrance. I almost want to pull away because I'm afraid of what will happen if I truly have sex with her, but she makes the choice for me by wrapping her ankles around my hips.

The tightest heat I've ever experienced in my life embraces me, and I never want to leave.

I'm hers.

She's mine.

I pump my hips. I can't stop moving.

"Ryan," she whispers my name. "Yeah, just like that."

Like I could stop. "Just tell me what feels good."

"All of it. All of you."

Fuck, I love my best friend for giving me this moment—giving us this moment—and turning his head because he knows how much rides on this.

I can't stop my body from moving as I thrust faster, harder. She's screaming now, and we're both fucked because Haneul sure as hell knows what's going on in here, but I don't even care anymore. I don't. I can't, not when I feel her clench around me, her thighs tightening, her body pulsing. Nope, I can't.

She's mine now.

Nobody else's.

"Ah-Ri…" I barely get out her name. "Why do you feel so damn good?"

She flips me to my back in an impressive jiu-jitsu move that has me grinning against her, despite the fact that I'm falling apart—completely apart. "Because I'm yours."

"Mine." I scrape my hands down her back. "Promise me."

"Promise." Her lips part, and I groan, pushing into her one last time.

She collapses against me with a scream, my name on a moan and her lips parted, her breaths coming in fast pants.

I don't even try to cover the noise.

I finish after her.

And I know in my soul that this isn't the end. It's just the beginning of us. Of this group. Of everything.

And for the first time since my sister's death, I think about my future.

I smile.

I've found my smile again.

Chapter Fourteen

Ah-Ri

I can't believe I just slept with my old archnemesis—I also can't believe how much I want to do it again.

I should have left right after. Instead, I stayed with him, in his room, in his arms, and I can't find it in me to be sorry when I get up around five and try to leave the bed.

Ryan pulls me back. "No."

He's so warm. I want to stay. "We have practice and a freaking Showcase soon." I yawn. "I have to at least get some sleep."

My body feels sore from him.

I welcome it and finally pry myself away, then look over my shoulder. Huge mistake. He's shirtless, basically naked, and all I see is smooth skin, a perfect body, and his ruffled hair.

"Not fair," I grumble.

He leans up on his elbow. "What isn't?"

"You looking like a prince, lying there all sprawled out like a sex god."

"Sex god... Yeah, I like that way better than TD."

I burst out laughing, despite how exhausted I am. "That may be a favorite moment in my life."

He smiles. "Mine, too, but only because you stayed."

I frown. "Where else would I have run off to?"

He grips my hand. "Will you do me a favor?"

His eyes won't meet mine. Oh, shit, is it already going bad?

I nod. "Sure."

"Please keep taking care of yourself. Keep eating. Even if that means the whole pizza, okay?" His eyes are so intense that I'm a bit freaked out. "No matter what, please take care of yourself. Eat. Rest when you need to, and don't read the comments when we debut."

"The comments?" I frown. "You mean online?"

"Don't read them. At least not without me. All right?"

I'm a bit confused, though I know his sister died by suicide, so I nod my head and agree. "Never without you."

"Good." He falls back against the pillows. "Now leave before I try to kiss you again."

"Okay, TD." I laugh.

He throws a pillow at me. I barely dodge it and grab the rest of my clothes. By the time I leave his room, I'm exhausted and, of course, approached by Haneul, who has a cup of coffee ready in a to-go cup and everything.

His eyes appear concerned.

I take the coffee. "Am I going to get the speech now?"

"He's still broken," Haneul says. He's wearing black sweats with a matching beanie. It looks like he's been sweating, so he was clearly up running or working out. "But maybe you'll be the one to find the pieces and put them back together."

"He doesn't need rescuing," I say. "Or fixing. Sometimes, the reason we lose the pieces is because we have to build something new."

Haneul stares me down and then shakes his head. "We should have been friends a long time ago if that's the shit you can come up with at six in the morning."

I laugh. "Yeah, well, you've always hated me."

"No," he says quickly. "I didn't. Honestly, I liked teasing you because you were so damn cute when you got frustrated, so competitive. And you're right, I'm a spoiled little shit so it entertained me, but I also, um…" He blushes. "May have had a slight crush on you. Don't tell Ryan."

"Say what?" I shriek.

He cups a hand over my mouth. "Don't read into it. I'm over it. Honest. And no offense, but I think maybe your place is with the pieces you don't see as broken but whole. Maybe that's your role. And while you're adorable, we'd probably kill each other."

I laugh. "Probably."

"Take care of him."

"And the group." I nod.

He curses. "Don't even get me started on the group. We don't have enough time, and we're—"

"Going to be totally fine." I put a hand on his. "Just trust your group. We'll work our asses off. Promise."

"I know." He nods his head. "I know."

"Stay safe." I wink. "And, yay, see you in two hours."

Haneul lifts his coffee cup. "I'll bring more of this."

"Ah, you're my new favorite person."

"Heard that." Ryan stumbles out of his room.

Haneul looks around me at Ryan, then back at me. "Did a fight break out that I don't know about?"

Huh? I look over my shoulder.

Fingernail marks score Ryan's shoulders.

He looks down. "What?"

"Sorry," I whisper, completely embarrassed.

Haneul snorts out a laugh. "Please. He'll probably take a selfie just so he can stare at his sex wounds."

I wince. "Let's not call them that."

"Nah." Ryan shakes his head. "Let's just never have any of these conversations again. I'm going to shower."

"See ya, TD!" I call.

Haneul holds his hand up for a high-five.

I laugh. "Solidarity."

"See? You're perfect for him." He winks. "Also, let's kick ass."

"Agreed." I yawn again. "See ya soon."

"Bye, Ah-Ri."

I barely remember getting home. I'm so exhausted. But I take a quick power nap and think about the guy I'm dating, my new group, life, and wonder how it will all work out.

It has to, right?

It just has to.

Chapter Fifteen

Ryan

It feels like it's been weeks since I had Ah-Ri in my arms, when really, it's only been a handful of days.

Our Showcase was moved to a sooner date, which means that all we're doing is rehearsing day and night.

I sneak in a kiss here and there, but both of us decide to put the group first, which is basically like daily torture when I'm dancing with her.

I groan when we practice one of our numbers again. I envision pulling her sweatshirt off her body and then realize that it was a really bad idea when I have to excuse myself for a break.

We talk every day, all night.

I've never been more exhausted or excited to be dating someone, which is officially what I'm calling it. She's my person, and the more I get to know her, the more I thank my sister.

She's clearly putting in a good word for me in the afterlife, right?

I go to the restroom and splash some water on my face. The door opens behind me, and I look over my shoulder.

"Ah-Ri?" I ask.

She launches herself at me. We stumble back against the sink, our mouths fused together as we struggle to stay connected.

"I missed your taste," I say against her lips.

Her moan goes straight to my cock. "I missed your body."

I pin her against the wall, and her hands immediately go to my hair. She scrapes her nails on my scalp, and it feels so good that I almost drop her.

She reaches into my joggers and grips my dick.

I flinch, so sensitive that I'm afraid I might embarrass myself when a stall door opens.

I drop her on her ass but then immediately help her up.

Her eyes are wide.

Footsteps sound.

One step, two.

Shit, this is the end of us, isn't it?

Shit, shit, shit.

I'm too busy losing my mind to realize who it is until he turns around and crosses his arms.

"S-sookie?" Ah-Ri jumps a foot and tries to adjust her shirt while I'm frozen to the spot.

Sookie calmly washes his hands, fixes his hair beneath his grey beanie, then turns to me, his expression hard.

This is bad.

"Break her heart, and I'll kill you." His gaze moves from me to Ah-Ri and then back. "And don't let anyone find out, or you're completely fucked."

"Aware"—I swallow, my throat dry—"of that."

"And maybe check the stalls." He shakes his head. "Amateurs. At least meet with face masks on at a park or something. Not that I've ever done that…"

I tilt my head.

He laughs. "Oh, and"—he pats me on the back—"good to see you've got your smile back. She'd be proud."

I immediately want to cry.

I want to break.

My insides hurt, and my throat burns.

And then Ah-Ri grabs my hand and squeezes it.

"Thanks," I say to him, but I also feel like I say it to her.

"Sorry," Ah-Ri whispers under her breath later once we're walking back into the practice room.

I just laugh. "Yeah, I'm not."

"I miss you," she says as the music starts again, and Haneul and Jisoo start their dance sequence.

"I'm not going anywhere," I say. "Promise."

She nods.

And then we dance.

We dance until we both want to collapse. Until every inch of our bodies hurts.

Tradition has us all going back to the talent apartments, and, so far, we've been able to escape the media since Haneul and I are supposed to be on a bit of a break from things.

Nobody but the label knows we've formed a group, so nobody's waiting for a comeback.

Little do they know, they're about to get a debut.

I break out into a sweat all over again.

"No more stress," Jisoo announces once we all finish eating at the apartment. "Let's just watch a movie and relax. We have a few days before we fail, or, you know…do well."

"The countdown from hell," I announce.

"Soju." Haneul gets up. "I say we sleep in, then work our asses off. But tonight…tonight…" He shares a look with me. "We become whole. A whole group."

I'm a bit confused why he said it that way, then Ah-Ri grabs my hand and squeezes it again, and it feels right.

Hours later, and everything is spinning. "Sojuuuuuuuuuuuuuu."

"Why are you yelling?" Ah-Ri bursts out laughing.

"Because it's a funny word," Jisoo answers. "Sojuuuuuuuu." She stumbles over her words, then grabs another shot and tosses it back.

We're watching *Spiderman No Way Home.*

Haneul keeps asking questions, so we have to keep pausing the movie.

"But why is there suddenly a multiverse that Dr. Strange doesn't know about? I mean, he's supposed to be the most powerful," he asks.

"How are you even able to have this conversation with that much alcohol in your system?" I throw a pillow at him.

He dodges. "Dr. Strange has eshplaining to do."

"There it is." I laugh. "But you were close."

"If I was Dr. Stranger," Haneul says, not realizing that he no longer even has the name right, "I'd change time. Wouldn't you change time?"

I suddenly feel sick. "Yeah, I would."

"What would you change?" Jisoo asks, and then I see it click in her head. "I mean, I would probably change my awkward teenage years.

Anyway, we should go to sleep."

She's trying to get me out of answering.

"Her death," I say. "I would change her death. I would have done more."

The room goes silent.

Ah-Ri leans in. "Do you want to talk about it?"

"He doesn't talk about it," Haneul finally says.

"She left a note." I pour another shot. "Not for my parents, but for me. She said she couldn't do it anymore. She said she was sorry. And then she was just gone from this world, hopefully no longer in pain. At least that's the way I like to think of it, that she was at peace. That she *made* peace."

Ah-Ri leans in, resting her head on my shoulder. "What was in her note?"

I smile at that because even though it hurts, the note included something. I get up. "Be right back."

The room is still quiet when I return and put the note on the table.

Everyone stares at it.

Finally, Ah-Ri grabs it and starts to read, her eyes moving back and forth as she mouths the words.

"She wrote you a song." A tear slides down her cheek. "And she told you to make a co-ed group called MXD. Her dying wish,"—more tears fall onto the table and collide with the letter my sister left. They probably mix with the tears *I've* already shed on that piece of paper—"was for you to do something brave. Because she felt like she wasn't. Because she looked up to you. Because you were…" She collapses against me, bawling. "You were her hero."

"I don't feel heroic." I hold Ah-Ri close. "I feel like a failure. I feel like I'm doing this for me."

"No." Ah-Ri sobs. "You're doing this for her. And even if that means that you're doing it for you, that's still okay."

"My parents don't know everything," I confess. "They think I just want to form a group. To be famous, to be more. To distract myself."

"It is a distraction," Haneul says. "But it's a worthy one."

I nod.

Jisoo's been silent this entire time. With shaking fingers, she grabs the piece of paper and starts to cry silently. I'm shocked that she's so moved until she starts to talk.

"A girl, another trainee, was bullying me. Sari was my hero that day, she stood up for me. Told the girl to back off. Sometimes when I was sad, she'd share her lunch with me or encourage me. I know she was tired, but she was my inspiration." Her eyes meet mine. "I told myself I would be just like her one day with other trainees. That I'd help encourage rather than compete."

"That was her." I can barely find my voice. "She was the best."

The room falls silent.

Finally, Haneul stands. "Well, I think we finally have a real group name then."

I jerk my head up. "What?"

"MXD." He holds out his hand. "I say we change from MNE to MXD."

Ah-Ri stands and puts hers on top of his, followed by Jisoo. Finally, I place my shaking hand on theirs.

"Now, it's real." Haneul nods. "And we know what other song we debut with."

"Hers?" I ask, not sure I understand.

Haneul shares a look with me. "It's what Sari would have wanted. It's her final message. It's her hope. It's our future."

I try not to cry.

I fail as we all hug.

And later that night, when Ah-Ri stays and holds me, I finally realize the pieces that I was so terrified to pick up and acknowledge, were the ones I needed the entire time.

Maybe it's through pain, bleeding, and suffering that you mourn and are finally able to look at the sunrise and smile.

Chapter Sixteen

Ah-Ri

Showcase Day

It's been two weeks.

I'm terrified.

Everything that could go wrong, down to our soundcheck, has gone wrong. On top of that, Ryan's parents are in the audience, and when our label announced our debut, the world basically lost its mind.

We were trending worldwide on Twitter.

Sookie didn't exactly help since he started tweeting about it.

And, as promised, I didn't go look at comments, but I know it's going to be equally bad and good on social media.

Everyone's watching.

To make matters worse, CEO Siu is at the Showcase, backstage. They're all there to support us, but my nerves are stretched to the point where I wonder if I'm going to just pass out when the lights hit me onstage.

We're all wearing white. Part of the concept with this song from Ryan's sister was a second chance. Heaven. Hope.

I'm in a tight crop top, a white skirt, and boots. Jisoo has on a similar outfit, but she's wearing tight pants.

The guys are both in nearly see-through white shirts, which I'm sure will make the world go wild since they're so good-looking. Both of them even bleached their hair—Haneul went lighter, and Ryan took his as light as it would go. I'm still trying to get used to it.

I have grayish-white extensions in my hair, and Jisoo decided to just go with it and wear a blond wig.

All in all, we look like angels.

Though the guys still look fallen. And if Ryan keeps sending me those smirks, I'm going to lose it.

He comes up behind me after I'm done with makeup. I stare at him through the mirror, my nerves clearly apparent as he hugs me from behind. "Someone could see."

"Let them." He kisses the side of my neck. "Let them know that I found someone."

Tears start to form in my eyes, burning them. "Don't. Don't make me cry right now."

He laughs. "Sorry, I just saw you standing here and really think that maybe you're my angel. Maybe when we die, we leave someone other than a memory. Maybe we leave a blessing or a gift for the people we leave behind. Maybe we leave a treasure." His eyes meet mine. "My treasure's you."

I swipe my cheeks and cling to him. "And here I thought I was just your anti-fan."

"Well, then I guess I'll spend all my time convincing you to become part of my fan club. I heard we have openings."

I burst out laughing. "You're too charming, TD."

"Take it back." He laughs and spins me around.

"What? The charming part?"

He looks around and then presses a kiss to my mouth. "You know what part."

I hold up my fingers. "Is it a small part? I'm confused."

"If we didn't have to perform in the next twenty minutes, you'd be so dead right now."

"From TD?"

He starts tickling me.

Haneul comes around the corner and makes a gagging noise. "You guys need to lay off the PDA before someone snaps a picture."

We touch foreheads and break apart.

"Sorry," I say.

"Oh, I already have a billion. So just in case you were thinking of bailing on us today…" Haneul winks.

"Ah, once a bully, always a bully." I grin.

Jisoo suddenly comes around the corner and holds up her phone. "It's okay. I totally got him farting in his sleep."

"WHAT?" Haneul yells.

"Kidding." She winks. "I just wanted to see your…wait for it." She snaps a photo with her phone. "Yeah, probably going to save that for the grandkids."

"The hell?" Haneul yells.

"Oh, yeah, we're probably going to get married. You're my type." She winks. "Are we ready to do this?"

Haneul's jaw drops.

Instead of crying, I can't stop laughing.

Ryan slaps a shocked Haneul on the back. "Let's do this."

"I don't even like you!" he yells.

Jisoo nods her head. "Okay, sure."

He does a double-take. "I do like a woman who takes charge, though. Think you could handle me now that the shyness is gone after sweating by my side?"

"Duh." She keeps walking next to him, then reaches for his hand.

I smile again.

Craziest debut I could possibly imagine, but here we are, getting ready to stream worldwide on the stage.

We all hold hands.

The lights lower.

The music starts.

And I see it.

A girl with brown hair and red highlights, sitting near the stage, smiling up at us.

She looks exactly like Ryan.

I perform as if my life depends on it, maybe because I know hers ended because of the pressure and stress. This is, after all, not just for Ryan. Or for the rest of us. It's for her, too.

When we end our first song, I open my eyes and find the seat empty.

I look over at Ryan. He smiles at the seat and holds his microphone close before starting her song.

By the time we're done, people are openly crying.

We move onto the next song.

Hours later, after our live performances, we're all at the apartment, and I'm keeping my promise to not look at the comments online. I feel like we did good. I feel like we did the best we could.

Sookie's been blowing up my phone.

I finally answer it. "Hey, what's up?"

"I'm so proud to be your friend." That's all he says, then freaking hangs up and sends me a text message.

With it is a picture of him.

And Ryan's sister.

Kissing.

I gasp.

Ryan looks over and then falls off the couch. "What the hell?"

"They were dating!" I shriek.

Ryan scrambles to his knees and calls Sookie over and over again until he finally answers.

Apparently, Sari and Sookie were close or got close. He tried to help her, and this whole time, he blamed himself for not seeing the signs.

Ryan starts to cry.

And I sit and hold him.

Then the rest of the group surrounds him, and I realize that this was how I was supposed to debut all along.

With love.

With family.

With my MXD group.

Because life is too short not to accept something different, something scary. Something that may change your life forever.

Ryan grips my hand.

I squeeze it back.

And I swear I see her face again, smiling down at us.

Mission accomplished.

Epilogue

Ryan

One year later…

Had someone told me a year ago that I'd be dating my best friend, my once sworn enemy, and also looking at our newest music video hit over two hundred million views on YouTube, I would have laughed.

And yet, here we are.

I'm holding Ah-Ri's hand as we make dinner with Jisoo and Haneul. It seems the video gets more and more hits every few minutes.

"We did it." Haneul throws his fist into the air and then grabs Jisoo and starts kissing her. "And who really knew that people would love that we're all dating rather than creating a scandal of the century?"

Ah-Ri snorts.

Jisoo follows and raises her hand.

"Nope, I rebuke this," I add in. "We took a risk. You girls nearly gave us heart attacks when you did that live!"

Ah-Ri just shrugs and sips her red wine. "There will always be people who hate it, fans that hate it. But I think more and more idols are coming out with details about their private lives. It's too stressful to keep that kind of secret. I refuse to live that way."

Jisoo taps her glass against Ah-Ri's.

How did we get so lucky?

Haneul looks at me. I look at him. We share similar smiles, and I know he's thinking the same thing I am.

Our label is supportive of us and our decision since it's best to get ahead of the gossip and drama rather than behind it, and while it did send shockwaves through the industry, it's nice to know that we don't have to sneak around anymore.

I don't know what the future holds for MXD, but I do know what it holds for me, and she's currently holding Slytherin as he glares across the table. He's been treating me like I've done him dirty. Of course, Ah-Ri treats him like a king...

I glare at him as if to say he has to sleep in *his* bed tonight.

He hisses as if he can hear me.

I suddenly realize that while my life may not be perfect or normal, and I may have let my dad down countless times and will probably let Ah-Ri, myself, my friends, and my cat down more and fail at some things, I'll always come back from it stronger. Because I have MXD, and I have my sister's dream in the palm of my hand.

I swear I can hear Sari whisper, "*We did it.*"

And we did.

Together.

* * * *

Also from 1001 Dark Nights and Rachel Van Dyken, discover Mafia King, Provoke, Abandon, All Stars Fall, and Envy.

**If you need to talk to someone, here are some resources that are available all day, every day.
Please know you are not alone.**

The National Suicide Prevention Lifeline
The National Suicide Prevention Lifeline provides free and confidential emotional support to people in suicidal crisis or emotional distress.
Telephone: 1-800-273-8255
For Deaf & Hard of Hearing: 1-800-799-4889
Online chat: https://suicidepreventionlifeline.org

The National Eating Disorders Association (NEDA)
NEDA is the largest nonprofit organization dedicated to supporting individuals and families affected by eating disorders.
If you are in a crisis and need help immediately, text "NEDA" to 741741
Telephone: (800) 931-2237
Text: (800) 931-2237
Online chat: www.nationaleatingdisorders.org/helplinechat

Sign up for the 1001 Dark Nights Newsletter
and be entered to win a Tiffany Key necklace.

There's a contest every month!

Go to www.1001DarkNights.com to subscribe.

As a bonus, all subscribers can download
FIVE FREE exclusive books!

Discover 1001 Dark Nights Collection Nine

DRAGON UNBOUND by Donna Grant
A Dragon Kings Novella

NOTHING BUT INK by Carrie Ann Ryan
A Montgomery Ink: Fort Collins Novella

THE MASTERMIND by Dylan Allen
A Rivers Wilde Novella

JUST ONE WISH by Carly Phillips
A Kingston Family Novella

BEHIND CLOSED DOORS by Skye Warren
A Rochester Novella

GOSSAMER IN THE DARKNESS by Kristen Ashley
A Fantasyland Novella

THE CLOSE-UP by Kennedy Ryan
A Hollywood Renaissance Novella

DELIGHTED by Lexi Blake
A Masters and Mercenaries Novella

THE GRAVESIDE BAR AND GRILL by Darynda Jones
A Charley Davidson Novella

THE ANTI-FAN AND THE IDOL by Rachel Van Dyken
A My Summer In Seoul Novella

A VAMPIRE'S KISS by Rebecca Zanetti
A Dark Protectors/Rebels Novella

CHARMED BY YOU by J. Kenner
A Stark Security Novella

HIDE AND SEEK by Laura Kaye
A Blasphemy Novella

DESCEND TO DARKNESS by Heather Graham
A Krewe of Hunters Novella

BOND OF PASSION by Larissa Ione
A Demonica Novella

JUST WHAT I NEEDED by Kylie Scott
A Stage Dive Novella

Also from Blue Box Press

THE BAIT by C.W. Gortner and M.J. Rose

THE FASHION ORPHANS by Randy Susan Meyers and M.J. Rose

TAKING THE LEAP by Kristen Ashley
A River Rain Novel

SAPPHIRE SUNSET by Christopher Rice writing C. Travis Rice
A Sapphire Cove Novel

THE WAR OF TWO QUEENS by Jennifer L. Armentrout
A Blood and Ash Novel

THE MURDERS AT FLEAT HOUSE by Lucinda Riley

THE HEIST by C.W. Gortner and M.J. Rose

SAPPHIRE SPRING by Christopher Rice writing as C. Travis Rice
A Sapphire Cove Novel

MAKING THE MATCH by Kristen Ashley
A River Rain Novel

Discover More Rachel Van Dyken

Mafia King: A Mafia Royals Novella
By Rachel Van Dyken

One of the first rules they give you when you're undercover—never fall for the enemy.

I didn't just fall for the enemy.

I became what I was supposed to hate.

What's worse: I fell in love with one.

I live a double life, and both sides know it's only a matter of time before I'm forced to choose.

Rebirth through mafia blood.

Or death at the hands of the very government I swore to protect.

I have one more job before my time's up.

I just wish it was anything but babysitting a mafia princess who's half my size but knows how to pack such a brutal punch I worry about my ability to have children.

Tin's small but terrifying.

And I'm her new bodyguard while we all go on a much-needed vacation.

I just have to stick to the plan.

And remember rule number one.

And stop kissing her.

* * * *

Provoke: A Seaside Pictures Novella
By Rachel Van Dyken

The music industry called me a savant at age sixteen when I uploaded my first video and gained instant fame. And then Drew Amherst of Adrenaline became my mentor, and my career took off.

Everything was great.

Until tragedy struck, and I wondered if I'd ever be able to perform again. I fought back, but all it took was a falling light to bring it all back to the fore. So, I walked away. Because I knew it wasn't just stage fright. It was so much more.

The only problem?

Drew and the guys are counting on me. If I can't combat the crippling anxiety threatening to kill me, I might lose more than I ever dreamed of.

Enter Piper Rayne, life coach, with her bullshit about empowerment, rainbows, and butterflies. She smiles all the damn time, and I'm ninety-nine percent sure there's not a problem she can't solve.

Until me.

She was given twenty-one days to fix me. To make me see what's important. What's real. The problem is, all I can see now is her. The sexy woman who pushes me. Provokes me.

Only time will tell if she's able to do her job—and I can make her mine.

* * * *

Abandon: A Seaside Pictures Novella
By Rachel Van Dyken

It's not every day you're slapped on stage by two different women you've been dating for the last year.

I know what you're thinking. What sort of ballsy woman gets on stage and slaps a rockstar? Does nobody have self-control anymore? It may have been the talk of the Grammys.

Oh, yeah, forgot to mention that. I, Ty Cuban, was taken down by two psychotic women in front of the entire world. Lucky for us the audience thought it was part of the breakup song my band and I had just finished performing. I was thirty-three, hardly ready to settle down.

Except now it's getting forced on me. Seaside, Oregon. My bandmates were more than happy to settle down, dig their roots into the sand, and start popping out kids. Meanwhile I was still enjoying life.

Until now. Until my forced hiatus teaching freaking guitar lessons at the local studio for the next two months. Part of my punishment, do something for the community while I think deep thoughts about all my life choices.

Sixty days of hell.

It doesn't help that the other volunteer is a past flame that literally looks at me as if I've sold my soul to the devil. She has the voice of an angel and looks to kill—I would know, because she looks ready to kill me every second of every day. I broke her heart when we were on tour together a decade ago.

I'm ready to put the past behind us. She's ready to run me over with her car then stand on top of it and strum her guitar with glee.

Sixty days. I can do anything for sixty days. Including making the sexy Von Abigail fall for me all over again. This time for good.

Damn, maybe there's something in the water.

* * * *

All Stars Fall: A Seaside Pictures/Big Sky Novella
By Rachel Van Dyken

She *left*.
Two words I can't really get out of my head.
She left *us*.
Three more words that make it that much worse.
Three being another word I can't seem to wrap my mind around.

Three kids under the age of six, and she left because she missed it. Because her dream had never been to have a family, no, her dream had been to marry a rockstar and live the high life.

Moving my recording studio to Seaside Oregon seems like the best idea in the world right now especially since Seaside Oregon has turned into the place for celebrities to stay and raise families in between touring and producing. It would be lucrative to make the move, but I'm doing it for my kids because they need normal, they deserve normal. And me? Well, I just need a break and help, that too. I need a sitter and fast. Someone who won't flip me off when I ask them to sign an Iron Clad NDA, someone who won't sell our pictures to the press, and most of all? Someone who looks absolutely nothing like my ex-wife.

He's tall.
That was my first instinct when I saw the notorious Trevor Wood, drummer for the rock band Adrenaline, in the local coffee shop. He ordered a tall black coffee which made me smirk, and five minutes later I

somehow agreed to interview for a nanny position. I couldn't help it; the smaller one had gum stuck in her hair while the eldest was standing on his feet and asking where babies came from. He looked so pathetic, so damn sexy and pathetic that rather than be star-struck, I took pity. I knew though; I knew the minute I signed that NDA, the minute our fingers brushed and my body became insanely aware of how close he was—I was in dangerous territory, I just didn't know how dangerous until it was too late. Until I fell for the star and realized that no matter how high they are in the sky—they're still human and fall just as hard.

* * * *

Envy: An Eagle Elite Novella
By Rachel Van Dyken

Every family has rules, the mafia just has more....
Do not speak to the bosses unless spoken to.
Do not make eye contact unless you want to die.
And above all else, do not fall in love.
Renee Cassani's future is set.
Her betrothal is set.
Her life, after nannying for the five families for the summer, is set.
Somebody should have told Vic Colezan that.
He's a man who doesn't take no for an answer.
And he only wants one thing.
Her.
Somebody should have told Renee that her bodyguard needed as much discipline as the kids she was nannying.
Good thing Vic has a firm hand.

About Rachel Van Dyken

Rachel Van Dyken is the #1 New York Times, Wall Street Journal, and USA Today bestselling author of over 90 books ranging from contemporary romance to paranormal. With over four million copies sold, she's been featured in Forbes, US Weekly, and USA Today. Her books have been translated in more than 15 countries. She was one of the first romance authors to have a Kindle in Motion book through Amazon publishing and continues to strive to be on the cutting edge of the reader experience. She keeps her home in the Pacific Northwest with her husband, adorable sons, naked cat, and lazy dog.

You can connect with her on Facebook www.facebook.com/rachelvandyken or join her fan group Rachel's New Rockin Readers https://www.facebook.com/groups/RRRFanClub.

For more information, visit her website at http://rachelvandykenauthor.com.

Discover 1001 Dark Nights

MACIE by Susan Stoker ~ ENCHANTED by Lexi Blake ~ TAKE THE BRIDE by Carly Phillips ~ INDULGE ME by J. Kenner ~ THE KING by Jennifer L. Armentrout ~ QUIET MAN by Kristen Ashley ~ ABANDON by Rachel Van Dyken ~ THE OPEN DOOR by Laurelin Paige~ CLOSER by Kylie Scott ~ SOMETHING JUST LIKE THIS by Jennifer Probst ~ BLOOD NIGHT by Heather Graham ~ TWIST OF FATE by Jill Shalvis ~ MORE THAN PLEASURE YOU by Shayla Black ~ WONDER WITH ME by Kristen Proby ~ THE DARKEST ASSASSIN by Gena Showalter

COLLECTION EIGHT
DRAGON REVEALED by Donna Grant ~ CAPTURED IN INK by Carrie Ann Ryan ~ SECURING JANE by Susan Stoker ~ WILD WIND by Kristen Ashley ~ DARE TO TEASE by Carly Phillips ~ VAMPIRE by Rebecca Zanetti ~ MAFIA KING by Rachel Van Dyken ~ THE GRAVEDIGGER'S SON by Darynda Jones ~ FINALE by Skye Warren ~ MEMORIES OF YOU by J. Kenner ~ SLAYED BY DARKNESS by Alexandra Ivy ~ TREASURED by Lexi Blake ~ THE DAREDEVIL by Dylan Allen ~ BOND OF DESTINY by Larissa Ione ~ MORE THAN POSSESS YOU by Shayla Black ~ HAUNTED HOUSE by Heather Graham ~ MAN FOR ME by Laurelin Paige ~ THE RHYTHM METHOD by Kylie Scott ~ JONAH BENNETT by Tijan ~ CHANGE WITH ME by Kristen Proby ~ THE DARKEST DESTINY by Gena Showalter

Discover Blue Box Press
TAME ME by J. Kenner ~ TEMPT ME by J. Kenner ~ DAMIEN by J. Kenner ~ TEASE ME by J. Kenner ~ REAPER by Larissa Ione ~ THE SURRENDER GATE by Christopher Rice ~ SERVICING THE TARGET by Cherise Sinclair ~ THE LAKE OF LEARNING by Steve Berry and M.J. Rose ~ THE MUSEUM OF MYSTERIES by Steve Berry and M.J. Rose ~ TEASE ME by J. Kenner ~ FROM BLOOD AND ASH by Jennifer L. Armentrout ~ QUEEN MOVE by Kennedy Ryan ~ THE HOUSE OF LONG AGO by Steve Berry and M.J. Rose ~ THE BUTTERFLY ROOM by Lucinda Riley ~ A KINGDOM OF FLESH AND FIRE by Jennifer L. Armentrout ~ THE LAST TIARA by M.J. Rose ~ THE CROWN OF GILDED BONES by Jennifer L. Armentrout

~ THE MISSING SISTER by Lucinda Riley ~ THE END OF FOREVER by Steve Berry and M.J. Rose ~ THE STEAL by C. W. Gortner and M.J. Rose ~ CHASING SERENITY by Kristen Ashley ~ A SHADOW IN THE EMBER by Jennifer L. Armentrout

On Behalf of 1001 Dark Nights,

Liz Berry, M.J. Rose, and Jillian Stein would like to thank ~

Steve Berry
Doug Scofield
Benjamin Stein
Kim Guidroz
Social Butterfly PR
Asha Hossain
Chris Graham
Chelle Olson
Kasi Alexander
Jessica Saunders
Dylan Stockton
Kate Boggs
Richard Blake
and Simon Lipskar

Made in the USA
Middletown, DE
14 July 2022

69323080R00078